QUEEN OF ASHES

EMPIRE OF SHATTERED CROWNS

2

MAY FREIGHTER

Newburn

King Gilebert's
Stadium

Royal Ac

THE ROYAL PALACE

KING GEROME'S
CATHEDRAL

MERCHANTS QUARTER

QUEEN ATHELA'S
LIBRARY

DUKE'S MANOR

LIONHART
GUILD

VICTORY ARCH

NOBLES QUARTER

Y OF DANTE

MARKET STREET

DEDICATION

To the man of my dreams, the captor of my heart, and the holder of the house keys.

May you three never meet.

FOREWORD

This book is written in U.K. English.

Some spelling may be different to the U.S.

Author's website:

www.authormayfreighter.com

Interior and Exterior Illustration:

Cristal Designs

CONTENTS

ACKNOWLEDGMENTS

I would like to thank my wonderful husband for suffering through this book and the following ones in the series. You have no idea how much I appreciate your feedback and ideas.

Also, a massive thank you to Nancy Zee from Crystal Designs for being my cover designer and proofreader. Although, you did a lot more than just proofread the novel, ha-ha. You are a great friend, and I cannot thank you enough!

And lastly, thanks to my editor for butchering my work.

"Why am I still affected by her?"
– Thessian A. Hellios

1

THE GREY WOLF

THESSIAN

Twigs and snow crunched under Thessian's boots as he chased Lady Riga into the forest.

She ran at great speed. Like a true hunter, she expertly avoided the fallen branches and mounds of snow. Her blonde hair was like a beacon in the white vastness, guiding him to his destination.

They suddenly came to a halt.

Enclosed by ancient trees, Thessian scanned the surroundings for the Grey Wolf.

"Are you certain he went this way, Lady Riga?"

The child glanced at him with an indignant look. "His trail ends here."

Unease clenched Thessian's stomach. His eyes raked through every inch of the thick tree trunks.

Riga pointed upwards. "I see him. He is on that tree. Watching us."

Thessian frowned. *Why isn't the Grey Wolf attacking? Is it true he can use mind-control magic?*

Winding his fingers tighter around the hilt of his sword, he stepped closer to the tree. "Come down from there!"

Ants crawled up Thessian's spine when the man, almost twice his size in muscle, jumped off a high branch with cat-like ease.

The Grey Wolf lifted his head just enough for Thessian to see his eyes glowing silver under his hood. A mess of unkempt, dark-brown hair covered most of his facial features. He opened his mouth and produced sounds similar to human language, but not quite. Then, he cleared his throat and, in a gravelly voice, said, "Human. Leave. Girl. Stay."

"I cannot agree to that." Thessian moved to shield Lady Riga in case the ominous stranger attacked.

The Grey Wolf sniffed the air. "Her scent." His voice became more agitated. "Murderer child."

"Lady Riga, do you have any idea what he is talking about?"

She bit her lip and shook her head.

"Very well. Stay back," Thessian instructed over his shoulder.

With each step she took, the Grey Wolf's growl grew louder. His fingers elongated and turned into sharp claws. He ripped off his cloak, revealing pointed wolf ears while fur grew on his body at a rapid pace. Yet, his humanoid form did not change.

Thessian had never encountered a beastman. According to the historical records, they were eradicated almost a century ago during the expansion of the southern kingdoms. Because beastmen once lived in the Great Forest, they often clashed with the humans who came to cut down the trees. The surrounding kingdoms ended up making a pact to kill all beastmen, sparing none. Somehow, the Grey Wolf survived. He could even be the last of his kind.

The Grey Wolf gave Thessian little choice. He lunged at the prince with his claws, swiping at an increasingly rapid rate. Each claw was as strong as steel. The sword in Thessian's hand could be compared to a stick when fighting a member of the beastman tribe. No wonder nations had to unite to eliminate them. Thessian's fifteen years of sword training proved insufficient, as he was put on the defensive.

A quick swipe of a claw came from the left, and Thessian ducked down. Propelling his sword forward at the same time gave him the chance to push the beastman back enough to regain his fighting stance.

The Grey Wolf quickly changed tactics. From erratic attacks, his movements became more calculated. For each step to the side, the beastman followed. The prince's sword clashed with claws so sharp that they visibly damaged its edge. As the blade got blocked, the beastman quickly swung his second arm.

Thessian staggered backwards. His lungs ached from the laboured breathing. He did his best to avoid the claws aimed at his gut and neck. Before he knew it, his skin burned when the beastman's claws met with his thigh. Sharp pain reverberated through his body when he used that leg for balance. Without looking, he knew the bleeding was heavy.

"Why are you trying to attack Redford when you could live a quiet life?" Thessian asked, hoping it would distract his opponent enough for a direct attack.

"Humans. Revenge." He kicked Thessian in the chest, forcing him to fall on his back. Looming over him, the Grey Wolf blew out a heavy breath. Through his sharp-toothed mouth, he roared with the same agonized cry Thessian had heard before the battle.

"This way, beast!" Lady Riga shouted.

When the Grey Wolf looked up, a ball of flame collided with him. His remaining clothes and fur caught on fire, and he fell backwards, yowling. He rolled around, attempting to put the fire out.

Lady Riga ran over to Thessian. "Are you hurt badly, Your Grace? Can you make it back to the castle?"

"It hurts, but I can still walk."

With her support, he stood upright and pointed the tip of his blade at the neck of the beastman as the flames dwindled. It was never his intention to partake in extinguishing one of the last remnants of a race. His resolve wavered.

"Kill me. Human."

"Why are you doing this?"

The Grey Wolf's silver eyes held much grief. Thessian had seen plenty of humans with the same expression after they had lost a loved one to war. "Revenge."

"But why? It has been such a long time since the War of the Great Forest..."

"No forest. Recent."

Thessian kept his blade trained on the beastman's neck and pieced the information together. The Grey Wolf attacked Redford for revenge. He said Lady Riga smelled like the murderer or had the same scent. Whatever happened had to do with the Fournier family and their hunting hobby. And since the beastman seemed disinterested in the deaths of the ice wolves, it could only mean one thing.

"Lady Riga, do you know anyone in your family who recently killed a beastman during a hunt?"

She pursed her lips. "Not exactly."

"What do you mean?"

"I heard Papa fended off against a beastchild in the Hollow Mountains two months ago."

Thessian could not hide his disgust. "Why would he do that?"

Lady Riga avoided his gaze. "As you now know, Your Grace, beastmen are strong. I am sure it attacked Papa."

The Grey Wolf snarled, "Lies! Khaja weak."

No longer could Thessian bring himself to kill the beastman. "If you promise to leave Redford alone, I will spare your life."

The Grey Wolf's beastly appearance receded, leaving behind a man with animal ears and a dirt-covered face. "I. Die."

"I am giving you a chance to live, beastman."

"Kill me, human. No revenge. No life."

Lady Riga pushed Thessian aside. "As you wish, beast."

She did not hesitate even for a second before she enveloped the Grey Wolf in a swirling tornado of fire.

From inside the flames, a piercing roar reverberated throughout the forest. It startled the birds and faded into the eerie silence that followed. The flames eventually dispersed, leaving nothing but ashes behind.

Once his surprise faded, Thessian grabbed her by the arm. "Why did you do that?"

"He wanted to die, Your Grace. That is all the kindness I could show him." She lowered her head. "I apologise for laying a hand on you. Please feel free to punish me as you see fit." As she knelt in the snow, she asked, "Your Grace, I want to request that you keep this from Papa. He does not need to know why the Grey Wolf wished to harm our town."

"That is not for you to decide, Lady Riga."

"I will do anything!" she pleaded in her high-pitched voice. "Papa is a good man and a skilled hunter. He is everyone's hero in Redford. I cannot let the others know Papa may have caused this."

In a stern voice he often used on his soldiers, he asked, "Do you realise what you have done, Lady Riga? To hide the truth, you may have killed the last of the beastmen, destroying their kind for good. Are you willing to bear this cross for your father, who committed the wrong?"

She sniffled and wiped at her runny nose with her trembling hand. Bobbing her head made her blonde locks bounce. "I—I will bear it."

Thessian had no children of his own. His father taught him that adults must answer for their wrongdoings, not their offspring. Yet, he could not turn down such an honest plea.

His anger subsided, and he offered his hand. "Get up, Lady Riga. We must return and get my injury treated. Otherwise, you may have to explain to your father why I died on your watch."

She lifted her head; her lovely face covered in tears and snot. "You will keep this a secret?"

"You have my word."

She finally smiled. "I will lead the way, Your Grace!"

By the time they returned to the Redford castle, the ice wolves had retreated. Apparently, the death of the Grey Wolf had removed the submission effect the beastman possessed over other beasts.

Lord Fournier did not bother asking many questions as he and Lord Carrell helped Thessian to a guest room, where a physician looked at the prince's thigh.

Pushing the round spectacles up his long nose, the physician asked, "Your Grace, this is quite a deep wound. It will require a miracle from His Holiness or a high-ranking priest to fix this completely. In the meantime, I will do what I can and cauterize the wound."

"Please do."

Thessian let the physician work while he drank the pain relief medicine.

After the way the Church of the Holy Light treated Emilia, he wanted nothing to do with them and their miracles. The wound would leave a scar, and he would remember the choice he made today. Once he returned to Darkgate, he could employ a healing mage. In the meantime, he could use the salve meant for the Empire's royal family.

Thessian sighed as he remembered he had given the salve to Emilia. Asking for it back would be rude.

Sir Ian waited until the physician excused himself and left. "Your Highness, are you planning to remain here and recover?"

"No. We will leave after I rest briefly. Ask Lord Fournier to prepare a comfortable carriage. I cannot ride my horse in my current state."

Sir Ian bowed his head and left to complete his task.

The quiet made Thessian's eyelids grow heavy. He closed his eyes. When he opened them again, evening had claimed Redford.

Sitting up on the bed, he spotted Ian sleeping on the floor with a throwing knife hidden under his palm. A tray of food had been placed next to the bed. Assuming the meat pie and wine were for him, Thessian dug in, using the silver cutlery provided.

After a long battle, a meal was a godsend.

Ian stirred. Seeing Thessian through the slits of his eyes, he shot upright and clutched his head with a groan. "Your Highness, you are awake. I apologise for not waking you earlier. I did not wish to disturb your rest."

"Sir Ian, have a change of clothes prepared for me. Has Lord Fournier arranged for the carriage?"

"He did. Should I have the servants prepare anything while I fetch your clothes?"

"No need. We will leave once the sun rises."

"Understood."

While Ian was away, Thessian sat on the edge of the bed and tested his leg. The pain told him he would not be running around anytime soon.

Perhaps, after he returned to Newburn, he and Emilia could sit in wicker chairs and share their woes and battle scars while Laurence gave Thessian an earful for not taking him along.

The door creaked open, and Lady Riga stuck her head in. "Your Grace, I saw your servant leave and…"

"You wanted to know how I was doing?"

She slipped into the room. Closing the door behind her, she nodded.

"As you can see, my leg remains attached."

"I am glad you were not badly hurt." The young mage pursed her lips. "Will you not tell Papa about the Grey Wolf?"

"I gave you my word, have I not?"

She bobbed her head. Shifting her weight from one leg to the other, she asked, "Could you take me with you instead of Volga?"

Thessian arched a brow. "Why would you want to accompany me to a camp full of soldiers? The conditions are not suitable for a lady, even if you have slain a bear and some ice wolves."

Her cheeks turned pink. "I ask you to do this because I wish to repay my debt to you."

His heart clenched. Such a young child like her was seeking redemption. Although he believed she did not comprehend the gravity of her actions in the woods, he was proven wrong. Riga was no fool who lived a sheltered life.

"You owe no debt to me, Lady Riga. You may retire to your chambers and sleep soundly, knowing I will not use this information against you."

"That is not what I meant!" She sucked in a deep breath. Her small body trembled as she spoke. "Mama taught us to repay the kindness we receive, and I cannot remain here, knowing the wrong I did. You were right, Your Grace. I acted on my emotions without considering all options or what the outcome would be. Knowing that I may have killed the last beastman weighs heavy on my heart."

Thessian wanted to get up and pat her on the shoulder as he would do to a soldier under his command but refrained. "You did not know. It was I who spoke too harshly, Lady Riga. The ones truly responsible for the death of the beastmen are long gone and labelled as heroes in history books."

"I will go with you, regardless!"

Thessian ran a hand over his face. Much like her father, she refused to listen to reason and acted however she wanted. "As long as you receive approval from your parents, I will permit it. We need a mage in our ranks."

Her eyes sparkled with excitement. "I will tell Papa immediately." She was gone before he could add anything else.

Blowing out a sigh, he muttered out loud, "At least she is more manageable than Lady Volga... I hope."

At daybreak, Thessian struggled not to gape at the carriage provided by Lord Fournier. The Count's servants packed it full of supplies, ice wolf pelts, barrels of ale, and other paraphernalia.

Thessian couldn't believe that the carriage hadn't tipped over with so much weight. Adding three people on top would increase instability.

The lords stood outside the castle to see him off. Most appeared as drained as Thessian felt. Next to Lord Fournier, Lady Estelle Fournier was holding Volga back.

Lady Volga shouted at her younger sister, "Riga, you stole my place! I won the match, not you! You little goblin, when I get my hands on you, I will—"

The rest of her speech was muffled by Lady Estelle's hand.

Lord Fournier stepped forward and cleared his throat. He had a couple of bandages peeking out from under his sleeve. The fight with the wolves did not leave him unscathed. "Your Grace, are you certain you wish to leave so soon? You need to rest."

Thessian smiled at the man.

In a short amount of time, he grew to like Lord Fournier's straightforward manner. Whatever happened between him and the beastchild had to be a misunderstanding.

Thessian simply could not picture a great man and warrior, with so many children of his own, going off and killing a beastchild without a motive. Too bad Thessian would never get the opportunity to ask for an explanation.

"Thank you for your hospitality, Lord Fournier. I hope to see you in the capital soon," the prince said.

"I will visit Newburn in the coming weeks," Fournier admitted with a sour expression.

Thessian turned to Lord Carrell, who joined them quietly. "And you, Lord Carrell? Will you also be joining us?"

"Of course, Your Grace," Lord Carrell replied with a growing smile. "I cannot wait to see how beautiful our new monarch is."

Lord Fournier hugged Lady Riga tightly. Tears streamed down his face like a flood, and he grumbled over her tiny shoulder, "I cannot believe you are the first to be taken away from me, Riga. I wanted you to grow up bigger. Remember to drink plenty of milk. If anyone gives you a hard time, you have my permission to turn them into charcoal."

"I love you too, Papa." Riga fought her way out of her father's tight grip with no success. "Papa, I am suffocating."

Lord Fournier groaned and released her. He rested his hands on his hips. "Remember to visit during the harvest festival. And write me a letter every day."

Riga's face turned completely red. "Papa!"

Lady Estelle wrapped her arms around her daughter. She pulled back with much reluctance. "You must write two letters. One for me and one for your papa."

Riga lowered her head as she grumbled under her breath.

Her sisters laughed at her while Lord Fournier wiped his snot away with his index finger.

Lord Carrell patted Lord Fournier on the shoulder. "There, there, Edgar. She will be fine. It's not as if you are marrying her off."

Lord Fournier perked up at the mention of marriage. "Your Grace, should you choose to marry one of my daughters, you must tell me. With Riga, you may need to wait a few more years but—"

Thessian raised his hand to stop him. "We should be leaving."

Ian appeared next to Thessian and helped him get into the carriage. Lady Riga sat across from him, and Ian took the reins.

Finally, they were off to the good wishes of the Fournier family and friends.

10

2

A WHEELBARROW OF SURPRISES

EMILIA

Emilia awoke from another nightmare. The fabric of her nightgown clung to her sweaty skin. She sat up in bed and stared at her hands.

For a second, she thought they were covered in blood.

She scrambled out of bed and splashed cold water from a washbasin onto her face. Looking in the handheld mirror made her cringe. She had dark circles forming under her eyes, and her skin seemed unnaturally pale.

"What is going on? Shouldn't the death of King Gilebert and my brothers be the end of these nightmares? Why are they starting again?"

A rap on the door was followed by Ambrose's concerned voice. "Your Majesty, are you in there?"

"You may enter, Ambrose."

The maid gasped when she saw Emilia's face. She immediately lowered her head in shame. "I apologise for my rudeness."

"It is fine. I had the same reaction."

Ambrose lifted her head. "Are you ill? Should I summon the royal physician to check on you?"

Emilia felt a shiver running down the course of her body. She glanced at the state of her clothes and stripped out of her damp nightdress. "Prepare a bath and a change of clothes for morning sparring. In the meantime, hand me a gown."

Ambrose hurried around the room, busy with the preparations.

This gave Emilia time to think. She needed to get some sleep, but the thought of going back to her nightmare made her stomach churn.

Are the spirits of the dead haunting me?

She made sure to bury her family members on the consecrated ground.

So, why are they appearing in my dreams?

"Ambrose, do you know of any remedies to help me sleep without dreaming?"

"I know herbal recipes for inducing sleep and calming the mind, Your Majesty. I have also come upon a recipe for being able to control one's dreams, but I have yet to test them myself."

"Hmm. Best to leave it for now. Ask Benjamin if he has any suggestions."

"I will."

After a long bath and a shoulder massage from Ambrose, Emilia felt a lot better. At last, she could ditch her dresses for a pair of hunting trousers and a comfortable cotton shirt. She threw on a warm overcoat and rushed to Lionhart's office, now located in the tower she had once called home. Only the gods knew why he chose that hellhole out of all the available rooms in the palace.

Upon her arrival, she found her spymaster busy going through a mountain of letters equivalent to the stack she had in her office. The stone walls were covered in his scribbles and maps of the land. He must have been working throughout the night, as the smell of wax remained thick in the air even in the late morning.

She leaned her hip against the door frame and knocked on the wood. "Lionhart, how about a sparring session?"

He lifted his weary gaze from what he was reading. "Sparring with Your Majesty will get me killed if I so much as leave a scratch on you."

"It will be fine. I won't press charges, I promise."

"I am not worried about you, Emilia. It is your new dog I am concerned about."

"Clayton? Why? He is harmless for an assassin mage."

"He may act harmless around you, but the reputation of House Escariot wasn't built in a day. They are known to be the best of the best. Even I must be on guard with that man around."

As there was nowhere for his guests to sit, she opted to walk around the room and study the maps he had pinned to the walls. "You know, Clayton found Julio Grande."

He pretended to return to his work. "Why am I not surprised?"

She chuckled. "Come now, he did good work. As a member of our dysfunctional family, we should praise his resourcefulness."

"You have accepted him too quickly," Lionhart pointed out. "Had it not been for his curse, his blade may point at your throat. Assassins are tools for murder. They do not have a master, not truly."

Emilia kept quiet. As much as she felt responsible for Clayton's troublesome curse, she could never pity him or bring him too close to her heart. Trusting people too much had caused nothing but grief in her past life. Her current life was not much different.

"Pick up your sword, Lionhart, and I will see you at the training grounds in half an hour."

"I have too much work to get through."

She smirked and made her way to the door. "Do not keep your queen waiting!"

Emilia did not need to wait long.

Lionhart left the tower right after her encouragement, and they proceeded to the guards' training grounds.

From a distance, she spotted Dame Cali, who had three young knights lined up. The men did not look too happy to hear whatever she was saying.

One guard, who acted like a self-important noble, shouted, "This is not fair! You are Hellion swine! Why should we listen to your orders?"

Emilia was about to step forward when Lionhart stopped her. "Let's wait and see what the lady can do. She is, after all, Prince Thessian's knight."

"You have a point."

Emilia crossed her arms and waited patiently as the scene unfolded.

Cali listened to the soldiers' complaints as she pinched the bridge of her nose.

"See? She can't even talk back!" the rowdy soldier mocked.

The rest laughed.

Emilia sighed. "This is going nowhere—"

Cali lowered her arm when the laughter died down and pulled out her sword. She kicked the most talkative man in the chest hard enough to send him flying backwards.

He landed on his back and yelled, "What do you think you are doing?"

The air around Cali changed. Her body automatically shifted into a fighting stance.

From where Emilia stood, she could not see Cali's expression.

Any further protests the men had died down in their throats as fear crept into their eyes.

The two who were standing backed away while the one on the

14

floor scrambled to his feet.

"Speak again, Sir Bonett, and I will spill your guts all over this training ground!" Dame Cali pointed her sword at his throat. "Pick up your sword this instant. If you can win against this 'Hellion swine', you can become Guard Captain."

Sir Bonett drew his sword from his scabbard. "I would never lose to a woman!"

Cali did not reply. She went on the offensive and pushed forward with a powerful swing of her sword.

The young man barely defended himself against the onslaught of her blows. Emilia could tell his movements were merely last-second reactions to the incoming attacks. He never had a chance.

With each swing, his legs quivered like that of a newborn calf.

Emilia leant closer to Lionhart. "That Bonett fellow, is he related to Count Bonett? One of King Gilebert's loyalists?"

"I believe so," Lionhart replied.

"I think I will have him stationed at the Northern Watchtower."

Lionhart gave her a sideways glance. "You are quite cruel. He won't last a night with his skills."

"He will have his friends with him. They might survive a week against the trolls."

They laughed.

With Cali's next attack, Sir Bonett's sword flew out of his hands. He attempted to retrieve it when Cali kicked him in the back.

Sir Bonett landed on his stomach, and Cali stepped on his back, pressing her blade against his exposed neck.

"This swine won the duel. Are you going to continue causing a ruckus or return to your duties?"

"I-I will go back!"

As Cali walked away from him, Sir Bonett picked up his weapon and charged at her.

Before Emilia could warn Cali, the dame already had a dagger in her other hand. She ducked away from the incoming swing and plunged the dagger into Sir Bonett's upper thigh.

Bonett cried out like a kicked dog. His hold on the sword loosened, and he fell, cradling his leg.

The quiet duo reached for their swords.

Emilia took this opportunity to come forward. "Captain Louberte, what is going on here?"

Cali whipped around at the sound of Emilia's stern voice. She masterfully sheathed her sword and bowed. "I was disciplining the men, Your Majesty."

"Does that require sending them to the infirmary?"

Cali blushed. "Usually not."

Emilia approached the wounded soldier, who stood to attention with much effort. "What is your name?"

He kept his eyes trained on the dirt. "It is Rem Bonett. Fifth son of Lord Bonett, Your Majesty."

Up close, Emilia could tell Rem was somewhere between eighteen to twenty years of age. His short, custard-coloured hair and dull brown eyes seemed to match his square-jawed face. Though, compared to Clayton or Thessian, he was like a background character no one cared about. "What is it you are unhappy with? Is Captain Louberte not doing her job well?"

Rem briefly glanced at his friends. "She is not one of us, Your Majesty. We cannot trust an outsider who has invaded our lands."

"Do you realise it was I who gave her this assignment?"

"Yes…"

"Are you questioning my judgement?"

"I am not."

"What will you do now?" Emilia pressed.

He lowered his head. "I apologise for the harsh words I have spoken and for disobeying the captain's command. Please punish me as you see fit, Your Majesty."

Emilia smiled at Cali. "Send him to the infirmary for treatment. Once his leg recovers, I will station Rem Bonett and his friends at the Northern Watchtower."

Rem kept his head low. "Please rescind your order! Anything but that!"

Emilia's tone grew colder than the winter frost. "Do you refuse your assignment?"

"I-I would not dare, Your Majesty."

Pleased, Emilia strutted back to Lionhart's side. "Shall we get going? Seeing a fight made me excited."

"Since you have recovered, I won't go easy on you, Your Majesty."

Emilia frowned when she heard him use her title and then remembered they were in public.

She smirked. "Bring it on, teacher."

Lionhart kept his word. She had to take another bath after the workout he put her through. Her muscles wanted a break as much as she needed a cup of iced tea. So, she sat in her office with a teapot of lukewarm green tea.

She took a sip and grimaced.

Gross.

Maybe I could use Clayton as an ice machine?

She giggled at the silly image of a veteran assassin conjuring ice for a cup of iced tea on a summer's day or after a sweaty sparring session.

Yeah, he will definitely stab me.

She palmed her face and groaned. "Why can't I be a mage? Spearing people with giant icicles looks much cooler than using a dagger. The bickering lords would also take the hint and not complain as much."

With a hurried set of raps on the door, Sir Rowell came into the office. He wiped at his sweaty brow with a handkerchief.

"Your Majesty, there is a cross-dresser at the gate with a wheelbarrow, claiming to be here to see you. On my order, the soldiers have escorted him to the courtyard as I recalled seeing him at the palace before."

"Good job. He is an acquaintance of mine." Emilia got out of her seat. "Lead the way."

He guided her through the halls to the courtyard.

On the way, Emilia was spotted by Ambrose, who proceeded to follow close behind them.

One look at Ernesto told Emilia he had been through a lot. His dress was in tatters and covered in mud up to his hips. His wig and makeup were fit for a horror movie. He stood next to a wheelbarrow and protected it from the guards with his arms spread out. "Only Her Majesty can look inside!"

The guards looked at each other.

"Step aside!" Emilia ordered her guards.

They got out of her way, and she approached Ernesto. "What happened? You look as if a pack of wolves has been chasing you."

Ernesto blew out a heavy breath upon seeing her. "Lady Em, I mean, Your Majesty, you finally came! I thought I would need to keep these rude men away forever. They do not know how hard it was to lug this *huge* and *heavy* wheelbarrow across half of Newburn and in this weather, at that!" His arms shot up dramatically. "I thought I'd die!"

Emilia covered her smile with a cough and stepped close to a wooden wheelbarrow that had a dirty brown sheet draped over it. The wheelbarrow was almost as big as the hand-held carts used by the traders in the city. It amazed her that Ernesto lugged it across town without his slender arms falling off.

I guess he's stronger than he looks.

She jumped back when something moved beneath the sheet.

"What is in there?" she asked.

Ernesto came over.

Untying the edges of the sheet from the frame, he said, "I was about to explain. When your servant—wait, what was his name? The mysterious yet handsome one? Anyway, he went in when the duke was in the middle of a discussion with someone. Jehan and I heard a lot of fighting coming from inside the house. We thought it'd be prudent to join. And so—" he whipped the sheet off the wheelbarrow, exposing the unconscious bishop and duke who were a tangle of limbs, "—this happened."

Emilia burst out laughing. "What a tale!"

"Ernesto," Ambrose cut in. "What happened to Mister Jehan and

Lord Armel?"

Emilia's expression sobered. The time for enjoying the situation could wait.

Ernesto lowered his head. "They were fighting the duke's guards when I left. My job was to get to the palace as fast as my gorgeous legs could carry me." He clasped his hands together and pleaded, "Help Jehan, Your Majesty!"

Emilia nodded and spun around. "Sir Rowell, get Captain Louberte and ask her to escort these sleeping beauties to the dungeon. Keep them under strict guard and separated. When she is done, have her bring as many soldiers as she can to Sudest Street. Ambrose, arrange for a change of clothes for me. We will leave immediately."

Sir Laurence sauntered over with his hands folded behind his head. He looked as if he had not slept well, either. "What is this commotion about?" He saw Ernesto and took a half-step back. "Did I come at a bad time?"

"No," Emilia replied with a growing smile. "You came at the perfect time, Sir Laurence. You are coming with us. Bring your sword."

Ernesto asked, "Should I alert Lionhart?"

"No need. We can deal with this ourselves."

Emilia's mind raced as she quickly changed into a comfortable disguise in her bedchambers. She tied her hair into a ponytail and pulled on a hood.

Ambrose approached her, clad in similar adventurer attire, with a longbow and quiver full of arrows on her back. She pulled out a black mask with a raven carved into it. "I was going to wait until your birthday, Your Majesty, but the opportunity to give this to you presented itself early. Please wear this to hide your identity. Now that the citizens know your face, it is too dangerous for you outside of the palace with no guards."

Emilia caressed the intricate design of the porcelain mask. "It is beautiful, Ambrose. Thank you." She pulled Ambrose in for a hug.

"Yo-your Majesty?"

Emilia drew back and put on her new mask before Ambrose

could see her reddening face. She had not given a proper hug to anyone in a while. To some, the warmth of another human being was commonplace. Emilia's life in the new world deprived her of affection from her family to the point where she began forgetting what it felt like.

Through the eyeholes of the mask, she studied her hands in wonder. The warmth of Ambrose's body lingered on her palms.

"Shall we go, Your Majesty?"

"Yes. I am itching for a fight after losing so many times to Lionhart today."

3

QUEEN TO THE RESCUE

EMILIA

Emilia, Ambrose, and Laurence rode on horseback to Sudest Street as quickly as the animals would permit. Her hood barely stayed on with the whipping wind fighting against her.

Emilia's heart raced at the possibility she had sent Clayton to his death. He was a skilled assassin, but that did not mean he was invincible.

She gripped the reins as she mentally chastised herself.

"We are almost there," Ambrose announced.

They got close to their destination and tied their horses nearby to not alert the enemies to their presence.

Emilia turned to Ambrose. "Eliminate anyone who tries to escape. Laurence, you are coming with me. At the last count, there were sixty men, so perhaps I should send you in on your own—"

"Your Majesty, when will you let me off the hook for a single fib?" he grumbled.

"When it gets old, I think. We should not dilly-dally. Let's go!"

Ambrose split off from the group, leaving Emilia and Laurence to sneak up on the gloomy manor that was half-covered with ice. The windows had been barricaded and could not be used as a point of entry.

Outside the rusted front gate, someone transformed five men with their weapons raised into frozen statues. Blood splatter decorated the front door. Standing in the entryway, Emilia could hear a lot of grunting, followed by a loud thud coming from the belly of the manor.

"What a rude welcome! Do you not agree, Sir Laurence?" She looked around, noting the people who lived nearby hid behind their doors and shuttered windows to avoid trouble.

Not a soul was out on the street.

"Fighting men in tight spaces will make it hard to use our swords," he said. "I suggest we draw the enemies out and fight them in the open. If your friends are still alive, they will have an opportunity to get away."

"Excellent idea. Please be so kind as to lead the Duke's remaining guards outside while I search the house."

"You cannot seriously be considering going in alone!"

She patted him on the shoulder. "I will be fine as long as you do your part well."

Laurence stepped out of her reach with a look of disapproval. "His Highness will skin me alive if I let you go, Your Majesty."

"Exactly. I am a queen. Do not forget that. Since Prince Thessian is not here to stop me, and I outrank you, I suggest you consider your options quickly."

He was about to say something and groaned. "I will do my best."

She beamed at him but quickly realised that he could not see her expression behind her mask. "I will be off then. Do not die on me, Sir Laurence. Prince Thessian will be quite upset if you do."

"Yes, he might even hire a necromancer to raise me from the

dead. I am that irreplaceable to him."

Emilia chuckled. "Good luck."

She waved and stealthily made her way to the back of the manor.

The overgrown shrubbery and weeds made for an easy cover. As she progressed, the thuds from inside the mansion became more frequent. She hoped Jehan and Clayton were alright. Their deaths would not rest well on her conscience.

A tug on her cloak had her freeze.

She gripped her dagger and turned her head to find the material had caught on a root. Jerking her cloak away from the obstruction, she was once more reminded why modern-day superheroes avoided capes.

The second she got to the backdoor of the manor, she removed her cloak. Pressing her ear to the door, she listened for any movement.

Silence.

She tested the handle.

The door did not open.

No matter. She learned to pick locks from Lionhart. His skill set was more suited for an assassin than an exiled nobleman. She had to rethink her evaluation of people.

Emilia knelt on one knee and rummaged in her satchel for her lock-picking kit. She selected the tools she needed and played with the locking mechanism.

In the distance, she heard a loud banging followed by Laurence shouting obscenities.

The noise within the manor skyrocketed.

Over a dozen of heavy boots made their way towards the front door through the corridors.

Emilia smiled. Sir Laurence made for quite an excellent distraction. Enough to bring out most of Duke Malette's men.

The last pin of the lock set into the barrel, and the door unlocked. She pumped the air once as a victory celebration and snuck in.

Light on her feet, she assessed her new environment from the dark corner. The foul stench of sweat and smoke made her stomach tighten.

I guess sixty unwashed men do not smell like roses. They could have sprayed perfume or something…

Along her way, she came across ten more frozen soldiers, similar to the ones outside. The Duke's men covered most of the intact furniture in dirty pitchers and empty barrels of ale. Sleeping sacks lined the floors along with the storage chests of the soldiers.

Did the Duke snuggle with his men?

Emilia snickered. She would ask him later.

The thudding came from the cellar.

Following the suspicious pounding, she made her way down a flight of old wooden steps. With each step she took, she grimaced inside the mask as low creaking pierced her ears. Luckily, the noise produced below muffled her entrance.

When Emilia arrived, she spied four men using a log as a battering ram against a sturdy wooden door. Most of the door frame had given in to the assault. A few more hits, and it would come off.

Emilia contemplated starting with a witty line but held it in. During her training, Lionhart insisted that eliminating the enemy quietly would keep her alive for longer.

She did just that.

Emilia threw two daggers simultaneously. They lodged deep into the backs of her targets, an inch or two away from their hearts.

The men grunted in pain and spun around.

The remaining two dropped the log with a deafening thud.

A bull-necked man, who seemingly liked to eat his horses whole, walked around his wounded friends and picked up an axe big enough to make an executioner jealous.

The others reached for their shortswords.

"Hmm, that was unexpected…" She waved her hands while taking a step back. "How about we try this again, eh, gentlemen?"

"Get her!"

Malette's men charged.

Emilia scrambled back up the stairs. Her heart rattled in her chest as her legs carried her so fast through the hallways and out the back door, she thought she would learn to fly.

Once in the open, she pulled out her shortsword and waited.

And waited.

And waited some more.

"Where are they?" She nervously pinched her arm and hissed. "I am not dead. What is going on here?"

She inched her way back to the cellar. Adrenaline made her heartbeat sound like a drum in her head. Her hand gripped the hilt of her weapon so tight that her fingers ached.

Arriving once again at the entrance to the cellar, she saw the axe lodged in the wall, and the mountain-of-a-man refusing to let go. He blocked the others from scaling the stairs.

The duo that got wounded by her previously was on the floor, growing paler by the second.

"I swear to listen to Laurence's advice more often."

She ran down and plunged her sword into the axeman's neck. Pulling the blade out with a spray of blood, she moved up the steps in case he, too, decided that a mortal wound was all for show.

The axeman clutched at his throat before careening backwards and falling onto her only remaining opponent.

His comrade did not budge after that.

"Is he dead?" She descended, one cautious step at a time. Just in case, she stabbed the axeman in the chest, pushing the blade through and into the man below him.

A pained cry escaped the trapped man, which was followed by the eerie quiet.

Emilia lowered her mask and wiped at her sweaty forehead. "I need another bath."

"Lady Em, is that you?" Jehan's voice came from the gap in the door frame.

Goodness, I nearly forgot why I came here.

"Yes." She retrieved her daggers and wiped the blood off them with her handkerchief. "Are you and Lord Armel unhurt?"

"I'm fine, but yer servant needs treatment." Jehan pried open the door with a loud cry of the bent hinges. He carried out an unconscious Clayton who had multiple cuts on his arms and legs.

"His wounds do not seem fatal. How did he become

unconscious?" she asked.

"I believe he used t'much magic ta protect us. Once a mage runs out of mana, they faint."

She pointed to the stairs. "Go out the back door and head for the palace. Ask the royal physician to take a look at him."

"What about ya, Lady Em?"

"I have a knight to rescue." She smirked and secured her mask to her face.

Emilia followed the sounds of fighting back to Sir Laurence.

Over twenty men surrounded him.

Dead bodies lay on the road, most of which had an arrow piercing their skull or neck.

Emilia was filled with pride. *Ambrose did a good job.*

As for Sir Laurence, she trained her eyes on the stabbed or slashed bodies.

One. Two. He got two of them.

"Sir Laurence," she shouted, waving her sword in the air. "I believe you have been slacking off in my absence!"

The Duke's men turned their heads.

"Get that woman! She might know where His Grace is," a bearded, brutish man, who had Duke Malette's crest branded on his sword and armour, barked. He had to belong to the order of Malette's knights.

Another arrow pierced through the air and hit its target.

The man closest to the knight collapsed without making as much as a peep.

"Someone, get that cursed archer!" the knight yelled.

The men encasing Sir Laurence split into three uneven groups.

Emilia backed up a couple of steps. Fighting two men at a time was doable, three was hard, but six would leave her at a great disadvantage.

"Gentlemen, how about some tea and cake? We have a wonderful bakery here in Newburn. What was it called again?" She stealthily fished out a dagger from behind her back and threw it at the head of a man in the centre. "Ah, yes, Toasted Buns!"

With a dagger lodged deep in his eye socket, the soldier swayed and fell on the cobbled ground. His sword clattered next to him.

The rest did not give her another opportunity to make a second throw as they charged at her.

Emilia took on a stance to solidify her footing. She sucked in a steadying breath and, at the last minute, decided it would be best not to engage in a losing battle. Twirling on the spot, she sprinted towards the tight alleyways where they would be forced to come at her one at a time.

She jumped over a blockade of stacked crates and kept running until the alley became so narrow that she could just about use her shortsword.

Her pursuers had bulkier physiques under their armour and struggled to swing their weapons.

"You are but a cornered rat!" the man with a large scar down his chin grumbled, kicking away a broken basket that got in his way.

Behind her, she heard footsteps crunching on the light snow.

They surrounded her.

"Haven't you heard? Cornered rats are the hardest to kill."

It's now or never.

Emilia tightened her hold on the hilt of her sword and attacked Scar Face first. All she could do was reduce their numbers as fast as possible.

He dropped his sword and pulled out a dagger from the sheath on his belt. His smirk stretched his lips as he parried her attack.

She did not relent and went for his legs next.

It didn't work.

When she got too close, he kicked out, making her jump back.

Emilia glared at him as she nearly slipped on the snow. Scar Face was a much better fighter than she had expected.

The men behind her were inching closer. They had taken the hint from Scar Face and changed to their daggers.

"Come on, girl. Give it up and surrender. Our commander won't hurt you...much."

"As tempting as your invitation sounds, my good sir, I will have to decline." She buried the tip of her boot in the fluffy snow. "For a lady such as myself does not venture out with strange men after sunset."

She kicked up the snow, which made a perfect cover for her next attack.

While Scar Face was distracted, she rammed her shortsword into his thigh and blocked his incoming swing with her dagger.

"You see, I only tolerate two men in my life who enjoy bursting into my bedchambers at night, and they are much better looking than you lot."

As she stepped back, Scar Face's eyes burned with malice.

Leaving her sword in place, he hobbled towards her and attempted to stab her with his weapon. His swings picked up speed as his frustration increased.

Emilia barely avoided his attacks when her dagger flew out of her hand with his next strike. She felt a wall against her back and a cold blade brushing her throat.

"I would not mind accepting that invitation now," she said sweetly.

"For stabbing me, I should take a limb or two." Scar Face leant in until their faces were inches apart. His foul breath almost made her gag. "What do you think, girl?"

"I like my limbs attached, thank you very much."

The men laughed.

She didn't.

The sharp edge of his dagger pressed closer against her neck, and he reached for her mask.

Emilia swallowed a knot forming in her throat. *They will kill me on the spot if they find out I'm the Queen.*

A blur of black landed on top of Scar Face and slit his throat with a single movement.

The mysterious stranger pulled out multiple throwing knives from inside their cloak and threw them left and right at the same time.

The soldiers who were laughing a minute ago fell like dominoes with their expressions frozen in shock.

Emilia stared at the back of the lean figure, who rose to their full height and straightened their posture. They were about three inches taller than Emilia.

The person whipped around and went down on one knee, their face covered with the hood of their cloak.

"Isobelle of House Escariot greets Her Majesty the Queen."

Emilia's knees nearly gave way from relief. "You must be Lord Armel's sister. Thank you for saving me." She frowned. "How did you know it was me in this mask?"

As Isobelle lifted her head, two ocean-blue eyes were embedded on a face as pale and clear as that of an elven maiden. She was as beautiful as Clayton, perhaps more so. Even her voice was soft and ladylike. Sir Laurence would drool for a month if he saw Isobelle. He may even profess his undying love in a dramatic display of affection.

"We have members of House Escariot working at the palace, Your Majesty. One of them informed me of your departure to help my brother." Isobelle looked around. "Where is he? He should be protecting you."

"Your brother's mana was drained. I sent him to be treated at the palace."

Emilia felt awkward standing against the wall. She made her way to pick up her weapons, some of which she had to yank out of limp people.

Isobelle spoke behind Emilia. "It would appear your soldiers have arrived. I will take my leave."

Emilia whirled on the spot. "Wait! If you are here, who is guarding Juli—And she's gone."

Only then, Emilia heard Dame Cali shouting, "Your Majesty, we have finally found you!" She ran up to Emilia with her mouth forming plumes of steam in the cold air. "Are you hurt?"

"I am fine. How are Sir Laurence and Ambrose?"

"They took care of most of the duke's men before we got here. The survivors surrendered into our custody."

"Good. Investigate the manor and search for anything useful. Anyone who got hurt must receive treatment." Emilia wrinkled her nose when she smelled something foul. She took a whiff of her coat and gagged. It smelled as bad as Scar Face. "Let us head home. I desperately need another bath."

"Yes, Your Majesty."

4

THE YOUNG MAGE

THESSIAN

Half a day into their journey, the carriage rocked.

Riga slid off her seat, and Thessian caught her by the arm.

The carriage came to a halt.

Sir Ian appeared in the doorway. "Your Highness, the back wheel came off from the heavy load."

Thessian helped Riga find her footing in the slightly tilted carriage and jumped outside with a pained groan. Most of his weight had to be put on his good leg. Offering his hand to her, she climbed down the unfolded step.

"Are we near a town or a village?" Thessian asked.

"We passed a small village an hour ago, Your Highness," Sir Ian replied. "Should I make the trek and ask for help?"

Thessian rubbed his chin. The stubble there prickled his fingers. "Lady Riga, we should be nearing the edge of Lord Fournier's territory. Do you know of any villages that are not along the main road?"

She looked around and pointed north-east, towards the sky-reaching Hollow Mountains. "Papa often visited the Dragon Village with me. It is on the way to the Northern Watchtower. Should be twenty minutes by horse in that direction." She lowered her arm and wrapped the cloak tightly around her slight frame. "Many good people live there, but the mine has become quite dangerous since last summer. More trolls and bluecaps keep appearing."

"Is Lord Fournier unable to defeat them?"

"The mine is on the king's territory, Your Grace. To mine the Dragon's Heart, the miners must pay a special tax to the crown. Without the king's express permission, Papa cannot send his men."

The Dragon's Heart jewel was exclusively mined in Dante. An old legend stated that a fire-breathing dragon once guarded the Dante Kingdom and died in the northern mountains. From then on, the king renamed them: 'Hollow Mountains'.

The death of a guardian beast caused monsters to reappear in the land. That did not stop the king's search for the dragon's remains, where he discovered a new jewel. It was crimson, like blood, with an ethereal shimmer. One glimpse at it could bewitch a weak-willed man. Thessian's grandfather embedded one of the purest and largest Dragon's Hearts in his crown, which made other kingdoms envious.

Thessian finally nodded. With his injured leg, he could not travel on foot. They could leave the carriage behind and take the horses instead, or wait until a trading caravan passed by.

He glanced at the sky. Although they left early in the morning, it was already late afternoon. The sun would set in an hour or two, leaving them stuck in the cold.

"Ian, unfasten the horses and prepare the saddles. We will ride to the Dragon Village and ask for help."

"What about your condition? I believe it would be best if Your Highness and Lady Riga remain in the carriage and wait for my return."

Thessian paused for a moment. Riding a horse could hinder his recovery. "You are right. We would only slow you down. Go. We will stay here."

"Please rest well." Sir Ian bowed his head and walked back to the horses.

Riga stared at Thessian intently.

"Is there something on my face, my lady?"

She ducked her head and covered it with her hood. "I apologise for my rudeness, Your Grace. You are a lot less stubborn than Papa. He would take a horse and ride to the village, even if he was missing a leg. He is not good at being patient."

Thessian chuckled. He could certainly imagine Lord Fournier riding a horse without a limb.

"I think it is best to trust my subordinates." He motioned to the carriage door. "We should get back inside before you catch a cold."

"I agree. I could use fire magic, but I may burn the carriage down by accident..."

The pain in Thessian's thigh lessened once his weight was off his leg. He could not believe he ended up fighting a beastman. The Grey Wolf did not seem to be at full strength. Grief drove him to make many mistakes. Had they met at another time, under different circumstances, Thessian wondered if they could work together instead.

"Are you in a lot of pain, Your Grace?"

Thessian blinked away his reverie. There was no point in contemplating events that could not be reversed. "I am fine, Lady Riga. Thank you for your concern."

He heard hooves outside. Sir Ian had left for his mission.

"May I ask you a private question?"

Riga lowered her hood and neatly folded her hands in her lap. Her posture was flawless. Sometimes, she acted more like a lady than her sister, Taiga.

"Ask away. After all, I am now your subordinate, Your Grace."

"Other than fire magic, do you have a passive skill or perhaps another form of magic?"

"Not that I am aware. After I awakened as a fire mage, I have

33

not sensed another ability within me."

"What do you mean?"

As she spoke, she gesticulated with her words. "Magical awakening is similar to being struck by lightning. A lot of energy comes to you at once, and it affects the surrounding area. I was in the stables when my magic awakened. The explosion burned the horses. All of them had to be put down. Nothing of significance happened to me since."

"Is that why you believe you do not possess a second ability?"

"I appear to be stronger than the fire mages described in books Papa bought for me. Though my control is lacking when I get emotional."

He raised a brow. "You did well against the ice wolves."

The corner of her lips quirked upwards. "I was having fun."

"I see. Do you require further magical training?"

She began to fidget. "Sometimes, I lose control and cannot stop the flames…"

Lady Riga could easily burn down Thessian's camp in the middle of the night.

How is Lord Fournier's castle still standing?

"Thank you for sharing that information with me. I will do my best to find a suitable mage to train you."

Riga's expression brightened. "I am in your debt once more." She hesitated for a second. "May I ask you a question also?"

"What is it?"

"Why did you decide to conquer the Dante Kingdom? You own quite a sizeable territory in the south of the Hellion Empire. Why come here?"

Thessian half-expected questions about his choice of weapon or the knights who served him, not his motivations. "I may not be able to relay my desire in its entirety, but one day, I wish for all the continent to be united under one banner where merit comes before personal greed or connections. Dante is a stepping stone in that direction." He moved his aching leg into a better position. "The Hellion Empire has three princes. The emperor granted each of us a territory to control and improve. He will choose the next in line for the throne once our efforts satisfy him."

"So, Your Grace took over more lands for the Empire?"

What a perceptive young lady! "While my elder brother is using his economics knowledge to build a trading hub in the dukedom of Hellios, I can only do what I do best."

"What about Prince Kyros?"

Thessian knew nothing of what went on in Kyros' head. Having learned that his younger brother was busy bribing nobles to side with him was disconcerting. Aside from rumours of Kyros' frivolous spending on fashion and high taxes in Spiora duchy, Thessian had not seen his brother in years.

Is my brother truly an incapable ruler painted by the rumours or a scheming villain?

She shifted uncomfortably in her seat. "Did I ask something I was not supposed to?"

"No. I am simply unsure of how to answer you."

"Papa told me Prince Kyros is not worthy of the Hellion's throne. He cannot fight, and he is not smart. He would bring ruin to the Empire."

"Lord Fournier seems to share his opinions freely."

Her cheeks turned red. "I apologise for my —"

He waved her apology away. "No need. I am glad to know he would speak his mind in any situation."

They spent the next two hours talking about her childhood and how magic had changed the way others saw her. While her family treated her no differently, the people in Redford were uneasy. They kept their distance and whispered about the stables incident behind her back.

Thessian could not help but feel a sliver of pity for Lady Riga. Many mages awakened before the age of twenty. Becoming one at nine seemed too cruel, especially when no other mages were around to teach her how to control her abilities. Riga had to do everything on her own.

For that, Thessian respected her.

The sun set and the air became much colder. The chill crept into the carriage, forcing Thessian and Riga to use the ice wolf pelts as blankets. A dancing light of a candle came from the lantern planted on a seat next to Thessian.

"I hear horses," Riga muttered.

All Thessian could see of her was the top of her blonde head buried in the white fur.

He strained his ears, finally picking out the same sound. He smiled.

"At last! I thought we would turn into ice statues before Ian returned." He removed the wolf pelt from around his shoulders. "I must thank your father for this wonderful gift."

"It will please him to know you like it."

A moment later, three horses halted outside.

Thessian clambered out of the carriage, careful not to put too much strain on his aching leg. The more he used it, the greater the pain became. He needed to find a healer as soon as possible.

Sir Ian bowed low. "I apologise for the delay, my lord. I have brought some craftsmen who said they could help us fix the wheel."

Thessian observed the older gentlemen, wearing thick fur coats and leather boots. Their horses had large leather satchels strapped to their sides, where he assumed they kept their tools.

Outstretching his hand to them, Thessian said, "Thank you for coming to our aid, good sirs."

The first man, who had a bushy grey moustache and an unkempt beard that reached his chest, shook hands with Thessian. "Naw need for thanks, milord. Naw one wants t'be stuck out 'ere in dis weatha."

"I can see why yer stuck," the second man grumbled, hopping off his horse. His boots sunk into the snow under his generous weight. He adjusted his fur coat and pointed at the carriage. "There's t'much stuff der."

"Must be travellin' pedlars, eh, milord?" the first asked without waiting for a reply.

"Naw," the second man interjected swiftly. "Don't seem like it, Freid. They'd have a cart."

Freid brushed his thick moustache and nodded with vigour. "I see. Foolish me. Where'd I be withoot ye, Gard?"

"Prob'ly in a ditch sum'ere."

They both laughed.

Thessian stared at them blankly.

Sir Ian whispered in Thessian's ear, "They were the only ones willing to help."

"I can see why it took two hours." Thessian spoke low.

"What's dat?" Freid asked.

Thessian changed the subject. "How long do you think it would take to fix the wheel?"

"It's gettin' too dark." Freid turned to Gard. "Think we shood leave it for 'morrow?"

"Ye, tha'd be best. Don't want 'em monsters comin' and takin' a bite oota me." Gard placed his hands under his round belly and jiggled it.

Thessian ran a hand down his face. "Excuse me, does this mean you will not fix the wheel?"

"That'd be correct, milord," Freid responded.

"We cannot spend the night out here. We have a lady in the carriage," Thessian insisted.

Freid glanced at the carriage. His face brightened when he saw the girl's face in the window. "Is that ye, Lady Riga?"

She opened the door and waved. "It has been a while, Mister Freid, Mister Gard."

Gard lumbered over to her. "Ye look grown-up, milady. Seems only yesteryear I crafted a bone dagger for ye."

"I carry it around even now." She pulled out a white dagger that seemed to be carved out of a beast's femur.

Gard grinned. "That be my dagger! I reinforced it with mithril. T'won't break easily."

She smiled and put it away. "Because of your beautiful craftsmanship, my first kill is always with me."

Despite the cold air that reddened their noses and cheeks, Gard's entire face and neck turned the shade of a beetroot.

Freid snorted. "Yer already married, Gard. Ye can't go fallin' for the yoong lady."

"Maybe in my next life den," Gard replied with a chuckle.

Thessian sighed. They had moved from one topic to another faster than he could keep up. "Mister Freid, is there an inn nearby where Lady Riga can rest for the night?"

"Just come back to tha Dragon Village with us. We can hide yer carriage in the trees o'er der." Freid pointed at the edge of the forest about a mile away from the main road.

In a restrained voice, Ian conveyed, "My lord is injured and needs to return to Newburn. I will protect you throughout the entire night as long as you fix the wheel."

Freid eyed Thessian and finally spotted his leg, on which he put little weight. "Sarry for keep'n ye standin', milord. Guess ye can't be ridin' horses, eh?" He sighed and approached the wheel. He grumbled a lot as he patted it and then kicked it twice. "Tha whole night, ye say? Shoodn't take dat long. What ye think, Gard?"

Gard made his way to the broken wheel and squatted in front of it. "We cood fox it in three hoors. Going back 'ome late wood be dangeroos."

"Ye, but yoong lady needs 'elp."

"Guess we must."

"Yeh. We must." Freid faced Thessian and Sir Ian. "We'll fox tha wheel for ye."

Thessian blew out a breath in relief. "Thank you, gentlemen. We will reward you handsomely for your assistance."

"Thanks, milord." Freid shuffled over to his horse and unstrapped the leather satchels.

After that, Freid and Gard got busy and only spoke when they needed a tool or for the lantern to be moved.

As promised, Freid and Gard completed their task within three hours. By then, darkness fell over the land and the nearby forest. As if to remedy that, the silver light of the moon reflected off the snow, making it glisten like a sea of diamonds.

"We're done 'ere," Gard announced and stretched. "Ye shood be fine for a while. Try not to o'erstuff yer carriage on yer next trip."

"We will." Next time, Thessian would have to decline Lord Fournier's generosity.

Lady Riga got out of the carriage and gave the craftsmen her handkerchiefs. "Please use this to wipe your sweat. You have worked hard for our sake."

Freid accepted the gift with a curt nod while Gard muttered his thanks.

Once Sir Ian paid the craftsmen for their trouble, they were once more on their way to Newburn.

Thessian reclined in his seat and closed his eyes. Despite being wrapped up in the ice wolf pelt, his shivering did not relent.

"Your Grace, your breathing is becoming uneven," Riga said with evident concern. "Are you feeling ill?"

"I will be fine once we reach the city."

She bit her lip and got up. "May I touch your forehead?"

Thessian raised a brow. He needed to hide his weaknesses better. "I have a low fever, Lady Riga. Nothing to worry about." Although he said that, he was fighting to keep his teeth from chattering and his hands from digging into his arms.

By the time Newburn was in sight, the interior of the carriage had become a blur and Lady Riga's voice a distant melody.

5

THE LONGEST NIGHT

EMILIA

After her third bath of the day, Emilia let Ambrose comb her hair while she sat in front of the dressing table. Thoughts clouded her mind.

Duke Malette is working with the bishop. Why?

It was no secret that the Church of the Holy Light believed her to be cursed.

Do they want to dethrone me, or is there another reason for their cooperation?

Ambrose's hand stilled in the middle of combing. "Your Majesty, why are you frowning so much?"

"I cannot figure out why Duke Malette is in bed with the bishop."

Ambrose gasped. "They *shared* a bed?"

Only then did Emilia recall that they did not use such a saying in her new world. "No. What I meant is that I do not understand why they are collaborating."

"Mister Lionhart will get the answers out of them."

"I asked him to question them, but physically torturing the bishop may cause a dispute with the Church. Lionhart can only threaten him."

Emilia got up and went to her bedside table, where she kept spare parchments and a fountain pen. She scribbled down a letter and melted some red wax to seal it. Then she used her signet ring to leave an impression on the hardening wax.

Handing it to Ambrose, she said, "Give this to Sir Rowell and have him send the letter to His Holiness via our most trusted messenger."

Ambrose kept stealing glances at Emilia's messy hair. "Should I finish brushing Your Majesty's hair first?"

"No need. I can do that myself."

With a hint of disappointment, Ambrose bowed and exited the room.

Emilia glanced in the mirror. Her complexion did not look any better than it did that morning. Two sleepless nights and days full of hard work had her running on fumes. As inviting as her bed appeared, she was not looking forward to another nightmare where she had to see her dead relatives.

Instead of combing her hair further, she arranged her raven locks into a single, thick braid. Her hairstyle might not be perfect, but it would do for a brief outing.

She left her bedchambers and made her way to the infirmary. It was her first time being there. The long room was filled with bookcases and had jars of liquids on every table. Almost like an afterthought, towards the end of the room, there were three beds, one of which was occupied. Next to it, Jehan had fallen asleep on a stool.

The royal physician, Benjamin Baudelaire, promptly arrived at her side. His beady eyes grew wide behind his specs when he saw her complexion.

"Your Majesty, do you feel unwell anywhere? Should I bring

you some herbs to improve your sleep?" He slapped himself on the forehead in a dramatic fashion. "I forgot that Head Maid Ambrose asked for some sleeping aid this morning."

"Never mind that. I am here for Lord Armel. How is he?"

The doctor pushed his round spectacles up his long nose. "He is in a deep sleep from mana exhaustion. I must admit, I am not very familiar with mage physiology. From my research, I believe he will recover shortly. I have applied a salve to the lacerations and bandaged his wounds."

"Did he sustain any serious injuries?"

"No, Your Majesty. Nothing I would consider fatal."

She smiled. "Thank you for your hard work, Benjamin."

"About your condi—"

"I shall visit the patient."

Emilia sauntered to the single bed where Clayton lay with his hands resting alongside his body.

The physician had taken off Clayton's shirt and bandaged his forearms.

She peeled back the blanket to assess the rest of the damage.

A wound on the side of his stomach was slathered with a green paste similar to the one Benjamin had used on her in the past.

Seeing Clayton hurt like that made her heart ache, and she stepped back. She made a rash decision to send him alone to retrieve the Duke. No matter the reputation of House Escariot, Clayton was one man.

In the future, she vowed to do better as his master and Queen. In addition to that, Emilia could have died had it not been for Lady Isobelle's timely rescue. She owed the siblings not only her life, but also her gratitude and respect.

Despite years of training with Lionhart, she was not skilled enough. In the end, her arrogance was the reason why things went downhill and almost ended up in tragedy. The people around her weren't mere characters in a novel. They were sentient beings with hopes, dreams, and free will. They felt pain and happiness just like her.

Jehan's bald head lolled to one side. He let out a loud snore, which startled him awake. Wiping at the drool on his chin, he blinked several times.

He shot up rod-straight when he saw Emilia. "Your Majesty, yer here?"

"I wanted to know how you and Lord Armel were doing. How do you feel, Jehan?"

"I've but a few cuts and bruises. It's nothing ta worry 'bout, Yer Majesty."

"You can relax around me. I am still the same person, just with a different title. After all, the guild members are my friends."

His stiff posture did not change. "Yer the Queen. T'would be impolite not ta acknowledge that."

"I guess you are right." Her lips curved into a wry smile. "There is no going back."

Clayton's breathing changed. He rolled his head to one side and ran a hand over his face.

Wincing, he opened his eyes. "Master?"

Emilia glided to his side. "I am glad you woke up. Are you in a lot of pain? Should I ask the physician to give you some pain relief?"

He attempted to sit, but she stopped him. "You have a nasty cut on your lower abdomen. You should stay still until it heals."

He chuckled. "Have you forgotten? I am a healing mage." He placed his hand over the salve, and a warm golden light emitted from his palm.

Ten minutes later, Clayton was sitting on the bed without as much as a single mark on him. In fact, his skin looked flawless, and she couldn't stop looking at his torso.

He won't notice me staring, right?

She hoped not.

I am just surprised by his healing abilities. That's all! Not like I haven't seen other guys without a shirt. It wasn't uncommon in her former world. *Nothing* to be bothered about.

Is it getting hot in here?

"I am all better," Clayton informed her with a bright smile. "No need to wear such a sour expression anymore, Your Majesty."

Emilia swallowed dry. "I-I am glad."

Jehan cleared his throat. "What about me? Will ya fix me up, too?"

"You do not look hurt to me," Clayton countered.

"Ungrateful scoundrel! If I hadn't gone in after ya, ya'd be dancing with tha celestials."

Getting off the bed, Clayton replied, "I would have managed on my own."

Jehan snorted. "Of course ya would."

Emilia balled her hands at her sides. Guilt replaced her embarrassment. The fate of so many lives was a heavy burden to carry. Rulers had to be heartless to sleep at night. But, she chose to support Thessian, because she did not want the people in her new world to suffer. It wasn't just about her survival. Not anymore.

She averted her gaze. "Lord Armel, I apologise for sending you in alone. I should have considered the situation better."

"There is nothing for you to apologise for, Your Majesty. I am your loyal dog. There is no order I will not execute if you command it."

A pang in her chest made her take a step back. He was not showing it externally, but his bitterness bled into his sharp words.

"Oi! No need ta blame Her Majesty for yer failures."

Suddenly, Clayton dropped to one knee in front of her and kept his head low. "I am sorry if I have offended you."

Emilia clenched her jaw and forced down her emotions. "Since everyone is feeling better, I should ask for an update from Lionhart. Good evening, gentlemen."

Without looking back, Emilia hurried out of the infirmary.

Each step felt heavier than the last. Her knuckles hurt with the effort she made to stop her hands from trembling.

"Dog? I never wished for a pet. They are too high maintenance. And what is wrong about being a dog? Dogs are cute." She ignored the protocol and rushed up the stairs. "Why is everything so far away in this palace? Teleportation—that's a useful skill."

The servants bowed when she hurried past, as if she had a horde of goblins chasing her.

Eventually, she arrived at her office and closed the door behind her. Tears stung her eyes. She blinked them away as she looked at the ceiling.

Queens do not cry.

Queens cannot show their weakness.

Emilia sucked in a deep, shaky breath, which helped push back her whirlpool of emotions. She was acting out of character.

Why am I emotional over what Clayton said?

She had no time to fall apart.

"This must be because of those terrible nightmares," she told herself.

A knock on the door made her jump. Good thing she was not in the middle of a crying fit.

She sniffled, rubbed her fingers under her eyes, and brushed down her dress before opening the door to find Clayton on the other side.

"Your Majesty, may I come in?"

He had a clean shirt on, making it easier for her to concentrate. Still, the shirt was too big on him, which indicated he had borrowed it from someone else.

Clearing her throat, she stepped aside and motioned for him to enter. With fake calm, she walked to her desk.

"I thought you had nothing else to report."

Clayton edged inside and closed the door.

He waited for her to sit first before joining her. "I wish to apologise once more for what I said back there."

"You weren't wrong. I am your master, and you are bound by an ancient curse to serve me. It was my fault for sending you to a dangerous place without having a clearer picture of the situation."

He placed his hand on his chest. "I chose Your Majesty as my master."

"You wouldn't if it were not for the curse…"

"I acted on impulse to prove my worth to you. I am the only one at fault for this failure. Please do not blame yourself."

"How can I not feel concerned when I have no—" She clammed up.

"No experience in being a ruthless ruler?"

"That too."

He smiled, and somehow, the weight of the world on her shoulders lessened. "Losing people is something you will have to deal with all your life."

"I know," she replied.

His smile grew wider.

"What is so amusing, Lord Armel?"

He shook his head. "You needn't be ruthless, Your Majesty. You just need to be your kind self and make your people happy. Look at the bigger picture, and do not concern yourself with pawns like me."

"How can I not when you and Jehan could have been killed?" The thought of losing two of her people left a bitter taste in her mouth.

"Our deaths would not be your fault. I should not have rushed in when I saw Bishop Lagarde. Instead, I should have asked my sister to send additional men. I—"

Emilia raised her hand. "Stop. As a leader, I have acknowledged my mistake. This is not a competition on who holds the most guilt."

"Indeed." Clayton swallowed nervously. "I hope you will not lose your faith in me after what happened."

"Of course not. You might have been reckless, but you were brave. Also, Lady Isobelle saved me today. Had it not been for her, I would have ended my reign as a monarch earlier than anyone else in the history of this continent."

"She did?" He raked his fingers through his raven hair, pushing the locks away from his handsome face. "Isobelle was supposed to monitor Julio." Frowning, he added, "Wait, why did you need saving?"

She started to fiddle with her paperwork. "Did Jehan not inform you?"

"I awoke not long ago. I have no idea how I managed to survive."

"You can thank Jehan and Ernesto. If it were not for them, I would not be aware of the situation you were in."

"Your Majesty came to my rescue?"

"Is that so hard to believe?"

"No. It was reckless," he rebuked.

She looked up, and their eyes met. "I guess, we are both reckless."

He chuckled but, suddenly, became serious. "What happened that you needed my sister's protection?"

She waved her hand in dismissal. "Let's not talk about that. All I need you to do is thank Lady Isobelle on my behalf when you see her."

"It is our job to keep you safe, even at the expense of our lives. No thanks needed."

She looked down at her slim fingers in her lap. So many lives were in her grasp. An entire kingdom depended on her. Sure, she was Queen in name only. Once Thessian reached his goal, she would be free to do as she pleased. Until then, she was bound with chains so heavy that they suffocated her.

"Is there anything else bothering Your Majesty?"

She looked at him. "You say it is your duty to protect me, but you cannot fulfil your duty when you are dead."

He considered her words in silence. "Will you feel better if I promise not to be reckless with my life in the future?"

She tilted her head to the side, "Will that be an empty promise?"

"I must be alive to protect you."

"Lady Isobelle did a great job in your stead…" she teased, hiding her smile.

"I am much better looking than she is," he joked.

She laughed. "I would not be so sure about that."

"Are you interested in women, Master?"

Taping her fingers on her desk, she demanded, "Does that matter?"

"Only for security reasons. I do not want you to escape my guard because of your sexual preferences."

Emilia covered her cheeks to cool them down. "This conversation is taking an unexpected turn."

"There are little secrets a master can hide from their servants.

Sooner or later, I'll find out about your lovers, your habits, and everything you like and dislike. You might as well tell me beforehand."

"I... Do not worry about my private life. I have no intention of taking a lover or marrying for politics."

Love? She was too busy surviving to even consider it. Having friends was already an upgrade from her former life. Falling for someone would be a liability.

"Your Majesty?" Clayton's voice brought her back from her reverie.

She focused on him. "Yes?"

"Is there anything else I can do to rectify my mistake?"

She decided to steer the conversation back to the interests of the crown. "We have Duke Malette in custody. Once his trial commences, he will be sentenced for high treason against the crown. In the meantime, rest. You have worked hard today."

"I feel uneasy resting when my master is suffering."

Taken aback, Emilia asked, "What makes you say that?"

"This may be rude to say, but you do not look well."

She faked a smile. "I've had some nightmares since the king's funeral. There is nothing to worry about."

"Have you had these nightmares before?"

"Never two days in a row. They feel so real when I dream that I—Oh, I do not want to bore you with the details."

He appeared thoughtful for a moment and rose from his seat. "I wish you a restful night, Your Majesty."

"Thank you, Lord Armel." As she was about to dismiss Clayton, Sir Laurence burst into her office.

"His Highness is back! And he has a terrible fever!"

Emilia was on her feet at once. "Where is he?"

Between ragged breaths, Laurence replied, "Ian is helping him to a guest room. Cali went to fetch the physician."

"Let us go together." She peered over her shoulder at Clayton. "Would you mind coming with us? I know you have recently recovered, but we may need a healer."

Clayton nodded.

They rushed to the room where Prince Thessian was lying on a four-poster bed. His pale complexion was worse than Emilia's.

She placed her hand on the prince's forehead. "He is burning up. What on earth happened to him?" She spotted a blonde girl who looked like a life-sized porcelain doll. "Who might you be, young lady?"

The girl curtsied flawlessly, even though she was wearing quite a heavy fur coat. "I am Riga Fournier, fifth daughter of Count Fournier."

"It is your queen you are speaking to, Lady Riga," Clayton corrected the girl.

Riga's eyes bulged. She ducked her head and bowed as low as she could in her curtsy. "Forgive my rudeness, Your Majesty. I did not realise who you were."

"We can deal with the introductions later," Emilia replied sternly. "Why is Prince Thessian in this state?"

"He was wounded during his fight with the Grey Wolf and refused to rest at my father's home to recuperate."

Emilia looked at Clayton. "Do you have enough mana to heal him?"

"I would need to see the wound first."

Laurence cut in, "Are you seriously considering allowing a death dealer to lay his hands on His Highness?"

Emilia had no time for arguments with Thessian's second-in-command. She spoke as diplomatically as she could. "Clayton is a healing mage. Why wouldn't I consider it?"

"He is an assassin!" Laurence spat out with distaste.

A lean man in a dark headscarf, who Emilia did not notice previously, peeled away from the wall and placed a hand on Laurence's shoulder. "We are all worried about His Highness. Do not let your feelings control you, Sir Laurence."

"If anything happens to him, I will kill you with my own two hands," Laurence snarled at Clayton and stormed out.

"I will speak with him," the knight said and went after his comrade.

Emilia thought the day would never end. From the onset, it was filled with trouble.

With a shake of her head, Emilia moved away from the bed. "Lord Armel, check Prince Thessian for wounds and heal him if possible. If not, wait for the physician and explain the situation to him."

"Understood," Clayton replied readily.

"And you, come with me." Emilia gestured for the girl to follow. She headed for the kitchen.

Not a soul was in sight as dinner had long since passed, and the chef and scullery maids were off duty.

"Are you hungry, Lady Riga?"

"Not at all, Your Majesty." The girl's stomach rumbled loudly, and she covered it with her hands. "I-I—"

"How about a nice omelette?"

Emilia searched the kitchen for the ingredients and a frying pan. Ever since she reincarnated, she hadn't cooked a meal. When she was a child, the maids would occasionally drop off some stale bread or vegetables, but they never brought her a proper meal. Once Ambrose joined her, and Emilia had her secret funds, Ambrose made certain to feed Emilia until her belly was ready to burst. Had Emilia not been doing her sword training every night, she probably wouldn't fit in through the door.

Emilia put the pan back on the wooden table and searched for a stove. Aside from a giant hole that looked like an unfinished fireplace, she didn't find one. "Well, this is odd. Where is it?"

"What are you looking for, Your Majesty?" The voice didn't belong to the kid.

Looking over her shoulder, Emilia spied Ambrose standing next to Lady Riga.

"Perfect timing. Where is the stove, Ambrose?"

"Your Majesty, please tell me you are not about to attempt cooking by yourself."

"Indeed, I am. Why? Do you think I would fail?"

Ambrose walked over to Emilia. "Please allow me to prepare a suitable meal for you and your guest. The kitchen is no place for a monarch. Your time is too precious to spend on watching ingredients bubble in a pot."

There was no arguing with Ambrose. Emilia had not cooked in over eighteen years. In college, she often used to eat ready meals and instant noodles. Those required little preparation. Here, everything had to be prepared from scratch. She could accidentally poison Lady Riga and face the risk of being murdered by Count Fournier, who was rumoured to be as tough as obsidian.

"You have a point. We will wait in the drawing room. Come along, Lady Riga." Emilia beamed at the girl. "I cannot wait to hear all about what happened in your father's territory."

6
PAST FAILURES

LAURENCE

Laurence stormed down the corridor and kept going until he reached the ugly statues in the garden. His fists ached to punch something. Anything.

How could Emilia let an assassin be in the presence of His Highness? What if he hurts Prince Thessian while pretending to heal him?

Unable to restrain himself, he hit a nude male statue, making its leg crack and fall off. The sting of his skin splitting over his knuckles and the tremor of the impact travelled up his arm.

He held in a groan.

Hanging his head, he muttered curses one after another.

"Are you planning to sulk all night?" It was unmistakably Ian's voice.

Laurence raised his head. *Why did the elf follow me?*

They were not friends. Ian was the kind of man who executed

orders without question or debate. The elf never let emotions get the better of him. On more than one occasion, Laurence wondered if Ian had any feelings at all. His expressionless face never changed and nothing was known of his background. Yet, His Highness accepted such a man into their elite ranks for his skills alone.

"Do not tell me you agree with the Queen on this?"

"I do if it helps the prince," Ian replied matter-of-factly. "If you believed she wished to harm His Highness even slightly, you would not have left his side, and your blade would point at her throat."

"Shut up!" Laurence hissed. "Now is the time you decide to talk up a storm? I think I prefer the silence you touted instead."

"Is that an order, Commander?"

Laurence rubbed his eyes and sucked in a breath of cold air that seemed to extinguish some of the raging fire in him. "No. I trust she would not do something as foolish as harming the prince. Her dog, on the other hand, is an unknown entity. He joined her side out of nowhere and claimed she was his master."

"Should we eliminate him?"

The two of them may be enough to take Clayton out.

It's not a bad idea.

But acting rashly could strain the working relationship between Emilia and Prince Thessian. Laurence had to tread carefully.

"Not yet."

Ian nodded.

"Listen, I owe you a pitcher of ale for this. Thank you for helping me clear my head."

Ian went back to being a man of few words.

Laurence should have used a memory crystal to record the moment Ian vocalised more than two words in a sentence. As it stood, no one at the camp would believe him if he told them what happened.

"I won't ask why you have failed in your guard duty, Ian. I assume His Highness told you to be elsewhere when he got hurt. Still, I cannot overlook this as your commanding officer. You are to return to camp and cook meals for everyone for a week."

Ian saluted him. "I shall take my leave."

"Remember, not *all* mushrooms are edible! We do not need the repeat of last year."

Laurence waited until Ian was gone and sat on a nearby bench. The cold from the stone quickly permeated through the material of his trousers.

He shivered as he longingly gazed at the starry sky above. "I am sorry, Eli."

Lawrence could not lose his head over his past failures, even if it hurt his pride. He jumped up.

"I guess it is time to go back." Laurence rubbed his itchy nose and sneezed. "Or it will be I who is bedridden."

7

TALL TALES

THESSIAN

Thessian peeled his heavy eyelids open. The feeling of being submerged under icy waters was gone, and his head no longer hurt as if someone rang a church bell in his skull. To his surprise, two unfamiliar faces stared back at him.

The man on the right was an older gentleman in his fifties. He wore round spectacles and had an air of clerical authority about him.

The younger man on the left, although he looked like he had not slept for days, wore a mask of caution and clear dislike.

"My lord," the older man said with a smile, "you are finally awake! I am Benjamin Baudelaire, the attending royal physician to Her Majesty."

Benjamin looked at the younger man and applauded. "Magic truly is a wonder. Had I the ability to heal others like you, Lord

Armel, my job would have been a thousand times easier."

With permission, Benjamin checked Thessian's pulse and assessed the leg wound, which was mostly healed.

"You are no longer in danger, my lord. Once Lord Armel recovers his mana, he should be able to heal the rest of your wound with ease." The physician took off his glasses and massaged his tired eyes with his thumb and index finger. "I will inform Her Majesty of your recovery if she is not asleep yet. Please remember to rest plenty."

Benjamin gathered his equipment into a leather bag and shuffled out of the room with a yawn.

"*Lord* Armel?" Thessian narrowed his eyes. "How come I do not remember seeing your name on the list of Dante's nobility?"

Lord Armel smirked as he stepped away from the bed. "The Queen ordered me to heal you with my magic. Are you not going to thank the man who saved your life, Your Highness?"

While the physician seemed oblivious to Thessian's real identity, Lord Armel was in the know.

Thessian sat up in bed. "I am thankful. Now answer my question."

Lord Armel reached into his pocket and fished out Thessian's protection amulet. "Here. I had to take this off to heal you." He tossed the amulet at Thessian, who caught it mid-air, and left the room.

A moment later, Laurence and Cali erupted into the room.

Laurence was the first to break the silence. "Your Highness, you scared us to death! If you died, who would pay me for these past two weeks of constant work and sleepless nights?"

Cali slapped her hand to her forehead. "Please ignore Sir Laurence, Your Highness. He was most worried about you. So worried, in fact, I heard he smashed a statue in the garden."

Laurence narrowed his eyes at her. "Did Ian tell you? That blabbermouth!"

"Actually, a guard saw the whole thing from a distance and reported it to me."

Thessian laughed. "I am pleased things worked out for the

better."

Laurence's expression turned sour. "I think you should know this. The man who healed you is an assassin who serves Emilia."

"Lord Armel?"

"Yes, him."

"That explains why he healed me, despite looking like he hated the thought of it. What do you make of him, Laurence?"

Through clenched teeth, Laurence replied, "He cannot be trusted."

Thessian had not seen that deep hatred on Laurence's face in a long time. Not since Sir Eli Godwin died protecting Thessian in Laurence's stead. All this time, Thessian hoped Laurence had moved on.

"Cali, leave us."

"I will return to my duties, Your Highness." She walked out of the room, quietly closing the door behind her.

"Have you not forgotten him yet?"

With a forced laugh, Laurence shrugged. "Whoever do you mean? I meet so many people, I cannot possibly recall them all."

"Drop the pretence. You know exactly who I am talking about."

Laurence's mask slipped away. The pain he had buried within the darkest part of his heart surfaced.

"How can I forget when it was I who asked Eli to trade guard duties with me? It should have been me who ended up dead, not him!"

Although his leg was mostly healed, Thessian felt discomfort because of the tightness in his muscles as he got out of bed.

He planted a hand on his friend's shoulder. "None of us had known an attempt on my life would happen that day."

Laurence scoffed and brushed Thessian's hand away. "As your second-in-command, I should have anticipated it. There was no way the King of Darkgate would give up without a scheme or two. Eli was ready to tie the knot. He told me about it almost every day, and I ruined his chance at happiness."

"It has been five years. No one blames you. We have won the war and returned victorious. Now, Darkgate belongs to us and the

Empire."

"Not all of us returned," Laurence said grimly.

There was nothing Thessian could say to make Laurence forgive himself for the past. He had lost many men during the war over the Darkgate Kingdom. Thousands of good soldiers were obliterated by the opposing forces because of his flawed orders or youthful indecision. He knew full well the weight of human life and how painful it was to lose a dear friend to the enemy. After all, he did his best to keep the deceased soldiers alive by visiting their graves once a year.

Faking a yawn, Laurence said, "It is late. You should rest while I stand guard outside."

"No. Take a break. You have been working too much recently. I see that now."

"Are you telling me to take time off?" Laurence stuck his pinkie in his ear and wiggled it around. "My ears must be full of wax."

"It is an order. Go back to camp and confirm my men have not frozen to death in our absence."

"Alright. Should they claim they feel cold, I will get them to run ten miles to warm them up."

"Before you go, give me an update on Emilia."

Laurence rubbed the back of his neck. "You may not believe it, but I think she may be suicidal. The people who work for her are crazy. This morning alone, a cross-dressing man came to the palace with the duke and a bishop in a cart. After that, she went off on a rescue mission, despite my warnings, forcing me to fight one hundred men on my own." Laurence placed his hand over his heart and shook his head dramatically. "I will have you know, I nearly died."

Thessian realised why the stories of Laurence and him were being exaggerated. He cocked his head to one side. "One hundred men?"

"Nothing can get past you, Your Highness. It was a jest. In reality, it was only forty men, and I had a maid with me. She was quite impressive, actually, and could fire three arrows at once."

"You expect me to believe you fought forty soldiers alongside a maid? Your tales are growing taller and bolder by the day."

"It's the truth!"

Thessian waved his knight's ramblings away. "You are dismissed. Get some rest as you appear to be hallucinating."

Grumbling something about unfairness under his breath, Laurence bowed and exited the room.

Thessian shook his head. *A maid who can fire three arrows at once? Who would believe that?*

The last person to visit him that night was Emilia. She came into the room looking as bad as Thessian felt. He kept his comments to himself, as she most likely was well aware of her appearance.

"Your Highness, I heard from my physician that you are no longer in danger." Emilia glided closer to the bed he sat on, with one of her steps faltering. She quickly covered her misstep with an adjusted posture and a smile. "How do you feel?"

"I am fine. Thank you for your concern. I apologise for causing such a scene."

"No need. This is technically your palace and your kingdom."

"What happened to Riga Fournier?"

Emilia's smile stretched. "The young lady is sleeping in a room I had Sir Rowell prepare. Your Highness, is this going to keep happening?"

He scrunched his brows together. "What is?"

"Every time you return from your travels, you bring a woman with you. Should I begin the construction of a harem? I must admit, Lady Riga is a little young..." She clapped her hands in mock excitement. "I know! How about a child-minding service for the ladies who have yet to reach the age of maturity?"

Thessian rubbed the back of his neck. "I did not initially plan on bringing her along. Things just worked out that way. Do you know any fire mages who could help her control her abilities?"

"She omitted the fact she was a mage during our meal," Emilia mumbled as she rubbed her chin. "Lord Armel is the only mage I know. I believe you've met. He is the one who healed your injury."

"The fake lord and assassin?"

"He is not a fake lord. Lord Armel is a Viscount and is officially employed as a judge in Count Jullien's territory."

"A judge and a death dealer? What an odd combination..." *How could a person who upholds the law also kill for money?*

Emilia swayed. "I must be tired."

Before she could collapse, Thessian lunged off the bed and caught her in his arms. She was so light that lifting her onto the bed required no effort.

"Emilia?" He gently shook her by the shoulders. "Wake up!"

She did not respond.

Thessian cursed out loud and searched for a pulse on her slim wrist. He relaxed when he felt a light, pulsating sensation under his fingertips.

"Wait for me." He rushed out of the room in search of the mage or her physician.

8

THE AMULET

THESSIAN

Thessian sat in a chair next to Emilia's bed, with his elbows resting on his knees and his chin on his knotted fingers.

Ambrose, who came out of a wall when he called for help, had moved her.

As if summoned by magic, Lord Armel also arrived in the Queen's bedchambers minutes after the maid lay Emilia down.

Benjamin tutted and pushed his glasses up his nose. "It would seem Her Majesty collapsed from exhaustion." He eyed Ambrose. "Head Maid, has she not been sleeping at night?"

"Her Majesty keeps having nightmares," Ambrose admitted, clenching her fists. "She wakes every morning drenched in sweat."

"How long has this been going on?" the royal physician pressed.

"As far as I am aware, since the funeral."

Emilia's breathing became laboured as she tossed and turned in her sleep.

Benjamin nudged the Queen's arm multiple times, even pinched it, but she did not startle from her night terror. "This is quite odd. Her Majesty should wake from the outside stimulus."

"We could pour some water on her and see if that works," Thessian suggested the remedy he used on his soldiers in the past.

"My lord, that is barbaric. If Her Majesty does not wake from such mistreatment, her body would grow cold, and she could catch a cold."

"I see," Thessian replied.

Lord Armel peeled away from the wall and moved to stand in front of Thessian. He stuck out his hand. "I need to borrow your amulet, Your Highness."

Unconsciously, Thessian's hand shot up to protect his magical amulet from the mage. "Why?"

"There is a theory I wish to test." Lord Armel motioned with his hand to urge the prince.

Once Thessian pulled the necklace over his head, he placed it in Lord Armel's awaiting palm.

Without a word of thanks, Lord Armel made his way to the Queen's bed and placed the necklace on her chest. It produced a powerful blue glow that indicated it had activated.

Benjamin gasped as he covered his eyes with his hands. "What is going on?"

Thessian rose from his seat. He squinted past the blue light that burned his irises. "Someone is using magic on Her Majesty."

"As I have suspected…" Lord Armel gave Emilia's hand a light squeeze and spoke to Ambrose. "I must leave Her Majesty's side for some time. Protect her well while I am gone. The dream weaver involved has to be hiding in the palace's vicinity or within its walls."

"Of course," Ambrose replied. "I will always be by her side."

Lord Armel started for the door when Thessian grabbed him by the arm. "Where are you going?"

"To find the monster responsible for my master's suffering!" The death glare Lord Armel fired at Thessian made him instantly let go.

Only then had Thessian noticed a glint of an ice blade that had appeared in the mage's right hand. Had he not released the mage in time, Thessian would be sporting another serious injury.

He returned to where the physician was gaping at the magical resonance of the amulet with amazement.

"How remarkable!" Benjamin reached for it, yet stopped midway. "Better not. Her Majesty needs it right now." He turned to Thessian, his eyes glistening with the curiosity of a child. "How did you come upon such an item, my lord?"

"It was a gift." Thessian's leg was aching again, so he went back to his seat. Once the weight was off his thigh, he felt much better and exhaled. "The mages at the Mage Assembly created that amulet."

"I wish I could meet such outstanding scholars one day." Benjamin's gaze kept returning to the pulsating blue glow given off by the necklace. "King Gilebert banned such items in the castle. The Church also frowns upon the use of magic and the existence of mages."

"Do you disagree with the Church of the Holy Light?"

"Nothing good will come from keeping people from knowledge. Had I known such items existed or how magic could affect Her Majesty's mind, I would not feel as useless as I did moments prior."

Ambrose sat on the edge of Emilia's bed and took hold of the Queen's hand. "You are not the only one who felt useless, Mister Benjamin."

The physician cleared his throat and nodded. "Her Majesty has stopped having her nightmare. Her body has relaxed, and she seems at peace." He bobbed his head as if confirming his words. "I will retire for the night and return first thing in the morning. Should anything else happen, summon me, Head Maid."

When Thessian was left alone with the maid and the sleeping queen, the room fell silent. He stretched in his seat and folded his arms over his chest. "So, are you Emilia's personal maid?"

Ambrose withdrew her hand from Emilia's and stood straight when facing him. She did not dare look him in the eye. "I am, Your Highness. I hope this does not offend you, but I believe you should return to the guest room. It is improper for an unwed woman and a gentleman to be in one room after dark."

"Ah, yes." He was uncertain if she was talking about herself or the Queen.

Regardless, Ambrose seemed to be the motherly kind—ready to throw an uninvited guest out the door. Her protectiveness of Emilia was similar to Lord Armel's.

He got up with a wince. His leg needed rest, as did his body, after the long couple of days. "I bid you good night, Miss Ambrose."

"Good night, Your Highness."

She escorted him to the door, once more making him feel as if he was being kicked out.

The door quietly clicked shut behind him, and Thessian sighed. "I suppose I should retire to my room."

9

THE DARKEST SCHEMES

EMILIA

For once, Emilia felt fully rested. She stretched out her arms and smiled.

No more nightmares!

A silver necklace with a round amulet engraved with magical runes fell onto her lap. She picked it up and studied its intricate design.

"Where did this come from?"

Next to the bed, she found Ambrose sleeping in a chair. Deciding not to wake her, Emilia slowly peeled back the quilt.

The sound of the shuffling bedding was enough to make Ambrose stir.

Rubbing her eyes, Ambrose asked, "How do you feel, Your Majesty?"

"I feel great!" Emilia grinned. "I could probably run for miles." She looked around, realising the last thing she recalled was visiting Prince Thessian. "My goodness, what happened?"

Ambrose's expression remained sombre. "You collapsed."

"I was quite tired last night..." She dangled the amulet in front of Ambrose. "And what is this?"

"Prince Thessian lent you his amulet to repel magical interference. Lord Armel said a dream weaver is involved in giving you nightmares."

"A dream weaver?"

"I have heard rumours about them from the guild members once. They are mages who can manipulate people's dreams or, in your case, create night terrors. Just like necromancers, they are demonised by the Church and disowned by the Mage Assembly."

"Why did one of them come after me? I do not recall hurting any mages in the past."

Ambrose shrugged. "Lord Armel left to find out. He said the dream weaver must be nearby."

Emilia had more questions, but chose not to torment Ambrose for much longer. She finally escaped her bed and got on with her morning routine. By the time she was dressed and smelling of rose oil, her stomach was causing a ruckus.

Ambrose finally let out a smile. "I will have the servants prepare a meal for you. Will you have it here or in the dining room?"

"The dining room. Check to see if Prince Thessian and Lady Riga are awake. I would like to invite them along. Have Lionhart attend as well."

"I will inquire, Your Majesty."

"Wonderful!" Emilia pulled open the doors to her balcony and stepped out into the beams of the morning sun. She sucked in a lungful of cool air and could not stop smiling.

She was no longer alone.

There were finally people in her life who cared, helped, and even worried about her. Such feelings were new and elating.

"Your Majesty!" Ambrose said sternly. "Please wear a coat when you are outside. The weather may be improving, but it is still the winter months."

Emilia waltzed back into her room with the skirts of her navy and gold dress flowing with her movements. "I cannot wait to hear what Lionhart got out of the bishop and Malette."

Within an hour, the food was ready, and Emilia sat at the head of the table. Prince Thessian was opposite of her, while Lionhart and Lady Riga sat next to Emilia.

Emilia had a napkin draped by Ambrose on her forearm, and Sir Rowell directed the servants with the food.

Reaching into her pocket, Emilia handed Ambrose the amulet. "Please return this to our guest."

Ambrose walked over and did as she was told.

With a frown, Thessian stared at the necklace in his palm. "Are you no longer in need of it? Has the dream weaver been caught?"

"Not yet," Emilia admitted. "I cannot dare part you with such an important amulet for too long. The mage may target you next."

"They seem more interested in you."

Lionhart sipped some of his wine and set his silver goblet down. "I would like to request for the servants to be dismissed, Your Majesty."

That could only mean one thing—Lionhart extracted information from the Duke or the Bishop, and it cannot be postponed anymore.

Emilia glanced at Sir Rowell and nodded once.

Once the food and drink were in place, the head butler ushered the servants out.

Ambrose remained to tend to Emilia's needs.

"Please tell us what you have found, Lionhart," Emilia urged.

Seeing him dressed as a proper gentleman was strange to Emilia. Yet, he was beginning to relax as his hair was tied loosely and the top two buttons of his shirt were undone.

Lionhart's cold, dark gaze landed on Lady Riga. "Where do your loyalties lie, my lady?"

Although young, Riga did not break eye contact with the spymaster. "I am a servant of His Grace, the Duke of Darkgate, Prince of the Hellion Empire, and the true ruler of the Dante Kingdom."

Lionhart chuckled. "What a long-winded way to say 'that man over there'."

Riga's face reddened. "I-I thought you wanted the full answer."

"Do not tease the girl," Thessian commented. "She can kill five ice wolves in one blow."

Lionhart let out a low whistle. "Powerful, indeed." He took on a more serious tone. "The Duke is adamant that he did nothing wrong by escaping his unjust confinement and that the assassination attempt had nothing to do with him, despite the assassin's testimony."

"It matters not what he claims," Emilia said, cutting into her fish fillet. "His trial is next week."

"The bishop remained completely silent until I took a snake out of a bag."

Emilia clenched her jaw to avoid having it drop open. "You jest."

"He wet his breeches at the sight of it."

Covering her laugh with her hand, Emilia's mood improved. After such an intense week, hearing that Bishop Lagarde finally got what was coming to him was great.

"Did he admit to anything?" Emilia asked.

"He said the dream weaver was supposed to drive you crazy, so Duke Malette could overthrow you on the basis of insanity."

Her grip on her knife tightened to the point where the

metal dug into her skin. "Those conniving pigs!"

Thessian crossed his arms over his chest. "We should have them beheaded for high treason before they hatch another despicable plot."

"I would love to, but I must wait to hear from His Holiness. Going against the Church directly would cost me, as I am seen as cursed by the people." Emilia lost her appetite at the thought of having to put up with more of the Church's politics. "I must have my coronation in a temple. All kings before me had it there, and I will too. That alone should show the citizens God has accepted me and dispel their fears."

Thessian leant in. "What if His Holiness refuses to cooperate?"

"He won't. The Church of the Holy Light is all about appearances. Their bishop conspired with a criminal to dethrone the rightful monarch. The other kingdoms will pull their support if the Church openly admits to engaging in such devious acts."

Lionhart added, "His Holiness will want to extradite the bishop to the City of Light."

"Should someone so vile be handed over, Your Majesty?" Lady Riga asked.

Emilia weighed her options. There was no choice if the pope wanted to take the bishop from her. She could not involve herself with the Church's internal dealings without power. And, as a monarch of a small kingdom, she was in no position to oppose them directly.

"You must never cling to things you cannot control, Lady Riga. In this case, I cannot control the Church. All I can do is negotiate a deal with them."

"Even the Queen can do nothing to them?" Riga lowered her head as she fiddled with her hands. "They dislike mages. Will they kill or exile me, too?"

"Do not fear, Lady Riga," Thessian said with a smile. "You are one of my people, which means you belong to the Empire."

In the original story, Thessian never had mages by his side. The people of the Empire saw him as a true hero who did not rely on magic to win his battles.

Would their opinion sway if he accepts mages into his ranks?

The people often hated their kind because of the teachings of the Church of the Holy Light. No wonder Lord Fournier kept his daughter's abilities hidden from Emilia's father.

King Gilebert hated magic and would have killed Riga or had her sent off to a faraway kingdom.

Does that mean Lord Fournier took a chance on Thessian not holding any prejudice towards mages?

Emilia could not allow the people's perception of Thessian to change if he was to rule the Empire. "Your Highness, I suggest you leave Lady Riga with me."

Thessian frowned. "May I ask for your reasoning?"

"It is simple. You mentioned she needs to learn control of her magic, and I know a mage who is adept at using his ability to its fullest."

"I have a nagging feeling that mage is Lord Armel," Thessian grumbled.

Emilia beamed at him. "The one and only. Once Lord Armel recovers his strength, I will ask him to become her mentor." She turned to the young girl. "Will that suit you, Lady Riga?"

"I will do as His Grace orders."

"I have no objections as long as he agrees to teach her *only* magic."

Emilia was unsure of what he meant exactly. Clayton seemed like the perfect fix to their problem. Riga would remain in the palace and learn control while Thessian kept the image of the perfect hero. Two birds, one stone.

"Shall we get on with our meal?" Lionhart commented and patted his stomach.

"Yes, we should." Emilia smiled. "Before I forget, Lord Armel has captured Julio Grande."

Thessian erupted out of his seat. "Where is he?"

Lionhart gritted his teeth. "That fox already knew of his whereabouts before our bet..."

"The food will get cold, Your Highness." Emilia smirked. "Enjoy your meal while thinking of what you are going to do to him."

10

A DISASTER OF SORTS

THESSIAN

After breakfast, Thessian followed Emilia to her office.

Once the door was closed behind them, he snapped, "Where is he?"

"Your Highness, don't you think it is improper to demand things from me in such a tone? I am not hiding Julio Grande from you." She lowered herself into her office chair and folded her arms over her desk. "I simply do not know where he is being kept. Once Lord Armel returns, I will have him escort Julio to you. Will that suffice?"

Thessian pinched the bridge of his nose and sucked in a deep breath. He had overreacted once again. Emilia, who was a decade younger than him, behaved as if she was the adult between them.

"I apologise for my rudeness."

"I understand how important capturing Julio is to you. Please take this moment of peace to recuperate. I can tell you are not entirely healed because you are limping."

"Lord Armel claimed he ran out of mana and could not finish healing me."

Emilia hesitated before saying, "Your Highness, you seem to have a great distrust of Lord Armel."

"It is because we are not on friendly terms."

"A pity. I thought you two would get along, since we are all on the same side."

"I do not believe he sees things in the same light as I do."

Emilia picked up a stack of parchments on her desk. "I must get back to work. Would you like a cup of tea before you leave?"

"No. I must head out to camp early."

She nodded and switched over to reading her paperwork.

As there was no more reason to remain at the palace, Thessian took his horse from the stables and rode towards his camp.

The whip of fresh air ruffled his hair as the sound of galloping hooves filled his ears. Nothing compared to the freedom of being outside of the stone walls of a palace.

He took the dirt path through the forest. Mountain ash trees reached for the sky, blocking out the weak rays of the sun with their tall trunks and casting thick shadows. The snow was melting, giving way to violet crocuses amid fallen tree branches. Soon, spring would be upon them.

He could not wait. Winter was beautiful, but invasions were best done in the summer. His men had suffered for following through with the coup in the last month of winter. The cold stayed strong, making them consume more supplies than usual.

Once the camp was in sight, he slowed his horse to a trot.

Smoke rose from the middle of the raised tents, making his heart beat nervously. He looked at the treeline on the right and the hills on the left.

No enemy forces or banners were visible.

The bad feeling continued to grow in his gut. He squeezed his thighs, urging the horse to pick up the pace.

Moments later, he arrived at the centre of the camp, where his soldiers were running back and forth with buckets.

He jumped off his horse, handing the reins to the nearest man, and followed the commotion. Pushing past the crowd, he was faced with black plumes of smoke rising from a cauldron they used to make meals for everybody. The stench of charred meat was impossible to miss as it burned the back of Thessian's throat.

"What is going on here?" he demanded.

His men quickly realised who he was and stood to attention.

Coughing, Laurence waded past the smoke and dragged Ian with him by the sleeve. "Your Highness, Ian messed up the food again!"

"Whose brilliant idea was it to make him cook? Have we not learned last time that disaster strikes when Ian is near a cooking pot?"

Laurence choked on his cough. "It was his punishment for failing to protect you."

"Ian, for ruining the cauldron and the ingredients, you are to run around camp until you can no longer move. Laurence, you will join him. Whoever is on cooking duty tomorrow will have to take over today."

The men cheered.

Laurence gaped at Thessian. "What happened to giving me time to rest and regain my energy? How will I come up with witty comebacks to keep you entertained if I am too tired to think?"

"It may be for the best," Thessian said with a nod. "Off you go." He fell into a coughing fit by accidentally inhaling the smoke again. "Someone, get this mess cleaned up!"

He strode to his tent and peeled back the door. As he entered, Ronne ran up to him.

"Your Highness, you have finally returned!"

"What is it?"

"I came to report. The Duke's men, who were camping outside of Newburn, have packed up their belongings and left, Your Highness."

Did they give up after hearing about Malette's imprisonment? "Did anything happen in particular?"

"I saw a messenger arriving shortly before they began to pack."

Thessian rubbed his jaw. "Which direction did they head in?"

"South. Towards Baron Niel's territory."

"Baron Niel is on our side."

In his tent, Thessian searched his chest for a map. He unfolded the parchment on his table and studied the nearby territories where the Duke's men could be headed. The territory bordering Baron Niel's from the south belonged to Count Alard. Alard was a staunch royalist and could not be Thessian's ally for the coup. After the king's death, Count Alard may have sided with the Duke. The Count's territory was at the heart of Dante and produced a lot of food for the kingdom. It was certain Count Alard was not short on gold and could fund a coup of his own if given enough time.

"Ronne, I want you to head to the palace and find a man named Lionhart. Report your findings to him."

Ronne placed a hand over his heart. "Yes, Your Highness."

Could the withdrawal have something to do with the assembling army in the south? Why would they leave? To confuse us? Or did they truly give up on the Duke?

His experience told him not to celebrate too early. He needed to know exactly what was going on in Malette's territory.

The sooner, the better.

For the rest of the day, Thessian made sure his men had everything they needed and were not short on supplies. Their supply route went through Marquess Carrell's and Count Fournier's northern territories. The time they needed to camp out was anyone's guess.

Thessian was not about to force his soldiers to remain homeless for more than three months. The coup was a success. All that remained was to solidify his regent's foothold. Later, they would focus on consolidating the territory with the Hellion Empire.

Splitting up his army in Darkgate and sending it to Dante could help eliminate uprisings but could weaken his dukedom.

As he walked back to his horse, his mind kept returning to the news he received that morning.

Laurence dragged his feet with sweat running down his red face. He approached Thessian and groaned loud enough to startle the nearby birds in the trees.

"I am done running, Your Highness."

"Where is Ian?"

Laurence glanced over his shoulder. "I thought he was right behind me." He shrugged one shoulder. "Who knows? Maybe he died of exhaustion."

"You should stop being facetious, Laurence."

"Lighten up, Your Highness." He pushed back his wet hair strands away from his face and shivered. "I should get changed before I catch a cold."

"Yes, you should."

Thessian grabbed hold of his horse's reins, put his foot in the stirrup, and pulled his body into the saddle. From the new height, he could see more of his camp and the way his soldiers aimlessly strolled around. Their eyes were missing the spark needed to win wars—the desire to fight. Thessian was not short on enemies, but the use of his men was not required yet.

"Do me a favour and run some drills with the men or get them to hunt the monsters in the vicinity. They seem listless."

"I will do my best to keep them entertained in your absence," Laurence said with a sweeping bow.

Thessian rolled his eyes. *How could I miss Laurence at Redford?*

"Get some rest, Laurence. I will be at the palace."

As Thessian rode away, he heard Laurence yelling after him, "I am overjoyed you care so much for me!"

With a twitch in his left eye, Thessian decided not to turn around and rode onward to his destination.

As Thessian got closer to the now-familiar castle gate, he greeted his knights on duty.

Their sour faces made him pause. "Is something bothering you two?"

Thessian climbed off his horse and held onto the reins.

Sir Leo Ritter and Dame Verena Vogel were always a team. While Leo took on the enemies with his spear, Verena focused on ranged attacks with her shortbow. She was not as skilled an archer as Ian, but she could fire at a rapid rate when needed. A fine team that had served under Thessian for as long as Dame Calithea Louberte.

Verena replaced her glum expression with a cheerful one. "It is nothing to worry about, Your Highness." She elbowed Leo in the side. "Right?"

"Of course!"

Thessian raised a brow. "It did not look like nothing. Give me the rundown?"

Verena lowered her gaze. "We did not wish to burden you with this, as it is a problem between soldiers. The tensions between our men and Count Baudelaire's are rising in the garrison. They continue to defy Dame Calithea's orders while belittling our skills. We have been courteous, but there is a limit to our patience."

A fight between the soldiers within the palace would cause an enormous problem, especially since Emilia's takeover as regent was still new.

"Do you believe Cali is unfit as Guard Captain?" Thessian asked.

Verena shook her head. "Of course not! She is a fine captain and always assigns duties with great care."

"What do you think, Leo?"

"I agree. It is not Cali's fault. Those Dante scum are the problem. They think they could easily beat us because we do not fight back."

"Mind your words, Leo," Thessian warned. "Dante will eventually join the Hellion Empire. Think of them as people of the Empire from this day forth."

Leo lowered his head in respect. "I will heed your order, Your Highness."

"Verena, has anything else happened?"

"I believe you should ask Calithea. She is in charge of the reports."

Thessian planted his hands on their shoulders. "Stop looking as if the world has ended. Guard duty will be over before you know it. Keep up the good work!"

They smiled and spoke in unison. "We will!"

11

MISSING

EMILIA

Emilia sat at her desk with the bridge of her nose pinched between her fingers. "Lord Armel, are you telling me your sister lost Julio?" Lifting her head, she eyed the siblings who kept their heads down.

Clayton slowly raised his head. "He got past our guard with help, Your Majesty. In truth, we had luck on our side when we caught him. Sightings of a man matching Julio's description among the servants were few and far between. With the commotion the funeral caused, we believe he surfaced to check on the situation only to be spotted by our informant in the west wing's halls."

Lady Isobelle dropped to her knees. "I am at fault! Please, Your Majesty, believe me when I say that I will take all the blame for this and accept any punishment. House Escariot does not forgive failures."

Emilia wasn't about to punish a band of assassins who willingly served her. That would cause them to hate her in the long run. Maybe, one day, she would end up on the other end of their sword.

"Rise, Lady Isobelle. It is not as if your brother has never made a mistake or two."

Clayton cringed while his sister's head shot up.

"What?" Isobelle's eyes were so large, Emilia thought they might pop out of her pretty head. "My perfect older brother made a blunder?" Her face melted into an evil grin that sent a chill down Emilia's back. "If Father was alive, he would whip Brother until he was half-dead."

Judging from Isobelle's words, Emilia was glad she had to deal with Clayton and not the previous head of the house. Not that she did not know how medieval mentalities worked when it came to physical punishment, but thinking that their father beat them, if they could not meet his expectations, was heartbreaking.

Next, Clayton fell to his knees, stopping her train of thought.

Emilia began to think they had practised their apology routine before coming to her office with the bad news.

"Your Majesty, I hoped I have rectified my mistake by capturing the dream weaver. He was hiding in the pantry at night to avoid being seen." Clayton pointed to the wiggling sack on the floor that Emilia was desperately trying to ignore since their arrival. "He admitted to working for Bishop Lagarde."

Emilia nearly snapped the fountain pen she was holding. "Why would a mage work for the Church? Don't they hate one another?"

"Not all mages despise them," he explained. "Some worship Luminos and believe they are great sinners for having awakened to magic."

"I suppose that makes sense."

There were plenty of cultists and extremists in Emilia's past life who put their religion above family or their livelihoods. Even in a fantasy world, people like that existed.

"Have him brought to the dungeon for further questioning," Emilia instructed. "As for Julio—"

"What about Julio?" Thessian asked as he opened the door.

Great. If the prince finds out about this, Clayton will fly out of the window.

Emilia put on her best smile. Before she responded, Lady Isobelle and her brother had weapons in their hands and were facing Thessian.

Where on earth did Isobelle hide that dagger? The female assassin wore tighter leather armour than the skin on Emilia's body.

Circling her desk, Emilia raised her hands. "Calm down, everyone. We are all friends here."

Unfazed, Thessian pressed, "Where is he?"

"He is indisposed," Emilia replied.

Thessian narrowed his eyes. "Indisposed where?" He glanced at the moving sack. "Is that him?"

"No. That is someone else." Emilia grabbed Clayton's and Isobelle's shoulders. "Lower your weapons. His Highness is the real master of this kingdom. You do not want to offend him."

Under her palm, Emilia felt Clayton growing tenser, but he melted his ice dagger as commanded.

Isobelle followed suit by sheathing her hunting knife behind her long, raven hair.

Emilia studied Isobelle's luscious locks with interest.

So, there is another use for long hair? Cool.

Thessian did not get distracted from his goal. "Please tell me you did not lose him."

"Of course not!" Gliding closer to the prince, Emilia spoke over her shoulder to Clayton. "Lord Armel, bring Julio here *as soon as possible*. I know you are keeping him at your *estate*, and it is a bit *far* from here. You need to hurry. Prince Thessian is eager to get his hands on this criminal."

Clayton must have understood her hint. He marched over to the wiggling sack and threw it over his shoulder. "We will retrieve Julio once we drop this off with the Guard Captain, Your Majesty." He paused in the doorway and added, "You have foul manners for a prince."

"You must be famished after a long day away," Emilia said to Thessian with a pleasant smile. "How about we have some dinner prepared for us?"

She drew Thessian's attention to her at last.

Looking down at her, he asked, "How did you know I would be hungry?"

"I assumed food cooked in the wild by a band of soldiers is not the best. What would you like? Sir Rowell mentioned we have boar meat in the pantry. I cannot wait to try it." She licked her lips. "Just as I cannot wait to try your secret brew."

Thessian slapped his hand to his forehead. "I forgot to bring a bottle with me."

"Are you certain you are not keeping it to yourself on purpose?"

He chuckled, no longer exuding the murderous aura that came out every time the topic steered towards Julio Grande. "I promise that was not my intention."

"I believe you." She looked at a painting of the late king on the farthest wall. "Ambrose."

After a soft click, the wall panel with the portrait opened.

Inside, with a lantern in hand, Ambrose stood with perfect nonchalance.

"Have a meal prepared for us."

"I will make the arrangements, Your Majesty." Ambrose backed out into the passageways, and the panel glided shut once more.

Emilia covered her laugh when she saw Thessian's stunned expression.

Turning his head to her, he asked, "Have you ever been told that you keep strange company?"

"Does that include you?"

He laughed. "I fear you are correct."

The servants prepared dinner within the hour.

According to Ambrose, Lady Riga planned to have her meal in her room and declined the invitation to join them.

While chewing on a rather stiff piece of boar meat in silence, Emilia itched to get out of the palace. The walls, the halls, and even the picturesque views from her balcony were becoming stifling. Although, she knew that the common people beyond those walls were living lives filled with hard labour and waking before the cockerel stirred. As tempting as it was to take Ambrose and ride off into the sunset, Emilia was a monarch. Her duty, albeit temporarily, was to her citizens.

"What have you on your mind?" Thessian asked across the table.

"Nothing that would interest you."

"Try me."

She set her cutlery down and wiped her mouth with a napkin. There wasn't a single smidgen of grease on her lips. Eating without the food getting on her face was one of the first etiquette lessons she perfected as a child. Walking gracefully was another matter. Without a mirror or someone to correct her posture, it was near impossible. At least until Ambrose arrived. With her secret maid around, Emilia got the kinks out of her royal walk, or as Emilia liked to call it—the royal shuffle.

"Tell me, Your Highness, what was life like at Hellion for you as a child?"

He rubbed his chin in thought and reclined in his seat. "It was busy."

"Could you elaborate?"

"I had sword training with the knights in the morning, then classes about the Empire's history and management, followed by a dance or etiquette class. In the evenings, Father liked for us to gather for a meal, so we were usually together." The upwards curving of his lips told Emilia how much he enjoyed those years.

"That sounds lovely."

"What about you?" He quickly seemed to realise what he had said. "I mean, did you have any hobbies?"

"There is no need to inch around my feelings. I am not so fragile that I would burst into tears at the mention of my past." Emilia took a sip of her wine and thought back to her younger days. "You know, I often woke at night, wondering if it was the day I would give up. On the quiet days, I would read at the tallest point of my tower, where golden sunlight filtered in through the only window that was not completely covered in dust. At my lowest, I knew that somewhere out there, a young man with fierce eyes as green as the Elder Forest's trees and hair as beautiful as gold was preparing to lead his men to battle for the first time."

She used the description of Thessian from the novel, as that was all she knew about him at the time.

Thessian nearly choked on his wine and spat it back into his goblet. "Are you talking about me?"

"Indeed."

His face reddened.

Ambrose quickly tidied the mess he had made and replaced his drink with a new one.

"I did not think you knew of my existence when you were a child. My first battle was at seventeen. I half expected to die there, along with my men."

"I know quite a lot about you. For example, I know that after your first kill, you silently cried in your tent all night."

Ambrose kept her head low and retreated to her place by the wall without making a sound.

Thessian cleared his throat and pushed his unfinished meal away. "Why do I feel as if I am here in my undergarments?" He nervously looked at Ambrose, who did not react.

Emilia giggled. "Ambrose won't speak a word of this. You have my word."

He rested his elbow on the table. "Since you appear to know all of my weak points, tell me some of yours."

"I could not possibly bore you with such dull conversation."

"Oh, believe me, I will not find it dull at all."

His wide grin made her swallow nervously.

Emilia downed the contents of her wineglass. Tempting as it was to tell him a bit about the suffering she endured throughout her two lifetimes, she didn't dare open her mouth. Eventually, their lives would take different roads. Giving him emotional ammunition that he could use against her would only bring her more tears later on.

"I have some matters to discuss with Lionhart." She got up. "I bid you a good evening."

Thessian's grin withered away. "Good evening to you as well."

Emilia could not bear to look at him. She strode out of the dining room as fast as the customs permitted.

Her hands balled at her sides when she created some distance between them. She stopped in the middle of an empty corridor and hung her head.

"Are you feeling unwell, Your Majesty?" Ambrose asked a few feet away.

Emilia shook her head. She was mad at herself for being weak and unable to fully trust those around her. She wanted to open up to someone. Anyone. Yet, every time she had the chance, the memories of multiple betrayals cut deeper and deeper. That lesson was carved into her soul, and she could not move past it. Not while she remained the same.

With each passing year, her shell hardened to the point where she saw people as moving mannequins. They walked and talked, all the while hiding their emotions behind their fake smiles and strategically formed sentences. Although she knew from the story that Thessian was honest and kind, now that he was a part of her life as a real person, she couldn't bring herself to confide in him.

What if he is not the same as in the book?

What if he lied to me like my professor at the university?

What if he betrays me, too?

Her skin crawled with ants as she recalled the jeers of her peers and the distrust of her parents.

Clutching her head, Emilia snapped, "Stop it. Stop it!"

"Your Majesty?"

A hand on Emilia's shoulder brought her back to reality. She turned her head and found Ambrose with a concerned look on her face.

Emilia managed a weak smile. "I-I am fine, Ambrose. Thank you."

"This may be bold of me to say, and you may punish me, but please rely on me more. It pains me to see you closing off your heart to everyone."

"Even you have noticed…"

"I have been by your side for years. Aside from menial tasks, you have never let me get too close, Your Majesty. Am I that untrustworthy?"

"That's not it! I trust you as much as I can. I just…need time. As for your punishment, please make me a cup of rose tea and have it brought to my office. I suddenly have a craving for it."

"Yes, Your Majesty."

When Ambrose was gone, Emilia walked to the nearest window and looked at the dark sky. The wind had picked up, harshly whipping the naked trees in the garden. Seeing those swaying, dark branches made her recall her nightmares.

"I should pay that dream weaver a visit."

12

LAURENCE'S SECRET ADVENTURE

LAURENCE

After a cold wash in the nearby stream, Laurence felt his sore limbs feeling slightly better. He dragged his feet to his tent, ready for a well-deserved nap.

As he approached his sleeping bag, he tossed his damp clothes onto his storage chest. He enjoyed some luxury due to his rank. Having a whole tent to himself was one of the perks. However, he seldom slept in his tent because he spent most of his time running errands for His Highness.

Flopping face-first onto the fur blanket, he muttered, "Thessian is a tyrant!"

His muscles relaxed, and he let out a long sigh. He should not have assigned Ian the cooking duty. Aside from it being Ian's punishment, Laurence simply wanted to see Ian's reaction. Instead, he ended up supervising a disaster in the making.

Who knew Ian would put sugar into the cauldron instead of salt and season the stew with jequirity?

Where did he find those seeds in the first place? It was not as if Dante was in a tropical region.

"Could it be on purpose?" He gave up on the idea. "After running all day, that elf cannot possibly look any better than I do."

From outside his tent, Laurence heard Sergey—one of the squad leaders—calling, "Commander, may I come in?"

Laurence reluctantly climbed to his feet and shuffled to the door. He peeled it back, saying, "Isn't it a bit late to be coming to my tent?"

The young man grinned. "The other squad leaders and I wanted to invite you to come with us. We heard from one of the passing merchants that there is a fine brothel hidden away in Newburn."

Laurence put on his best imitation of Prince Thessian's imposing demeanour. "Squad Leader Sergey Larvios, are you telling me you are planning an unsanctioned excursion into town to blow off some steam?"

Sergey stood to attention with his arms pressed to his sides. "Yes, Commander! That is exactly what I am saying."

Laurence grinned widely. "Count me in!"

His grin turned evil as he thought of a way to take a small revenge on Ian. Tonight, the stiff elf was going to learn to relax one way or another.

"Inform Sir Ian that he must come along. Under no circumstances are you to reveal where we are going." He got into Sergey's face. "Understood? Tell him we are on a secret mission for His Highness."

Sergey saluted him. "Yes, Commander."

In a hurry, Laurence sprayed the citrus perfume he purchased from a peddler onto his neck and wrists. It had been a hit with the noble women in Hellion and was sure to get him the best treatment at the brothel.

He found a clean shirt and donned it, along with his merchant's disguise. In a handheld silver mirror, he checked his dashing appearance.

He winked at his reflection.

So handsome, even I would fall for myself.

Twenty minutes later, Laurence rendezvoused with seven squad leaders and Sir Ian. They waited for him at the treeline where they tied the horses.

Ian did not seem too pleased about the sudden gathering. He rested his back against a tree with his arms and legs crossed.

Laurence walked over to him. "Why the long face? Are you not excited to receive a mission from His Highness?"

Ian glared at him.

"Do not fret. Even if your limbs are ready to fall off, you won't feel like that for long. Trust me."

"May I ask, what does our *mission* have to do with a brothel?"

Laurence glowered at Sergey over his shoulder. *That idiot forgot to warn the others in his excitement.*

Draping his arm over Sir Ian's shoulders, Laurence leant in. He kept his expression as serious as possible.

"The mission is to locate and subdue Julio Grande. We've received word he may be hiding in a brothel."

With a step forward, Ian shook off Laurence's arm. "I understand."

Laurence beamed at him. For once, he was glad Ian was not a chatty man. The elf accepted his orders with virtually no struggle, which made Laurence's job that much easier.

Laurence waved to the other squad leaders. "Off we go, men! This mission cannot wait for much longer."

They all cheered, except for Ian.

Laurence had underestimated how tired the muscles in his legs were. Riding a horse had proven to be quite an ordeal. Each gallop felt like a jab of a knife in his thighs.

Yet, he ventured on.

The desire to bury his face in the soft bosoms of a fiery redhead or a gentle brunette kept his spirit roaring despite the discomfort. He could almost feel the smooth skin of a woman against his hands and face. His only worry was that he may not satisfy enough ladies that night. Running took too much of his energy.

They secured their horses near Market Street in high spirits.

Laurence turned to Sergey. "Do you know where it is? The last time I strolled through the city, I found nothing that resembled a brothel."

"Worry not, Commander. The merchant told us it was a hidden gem in Newburn. Entry is restricted unless you know the passphrase, and all guests must wear masks at all times."

Laurence nodded thoughtfully. "It must be a brothel for the nobles if there are so many rules. It may even rival The Golden Suns!"

They grinned at each other.

To keep the act of a mission going, Laurence wiped the giddiness off his face and approached Ian. "Listen, the place where we are headed will require you to act like a customer. Do you think you can do that?"

Ian nodded once.

"Do you honestly understand what I am saying?"

Ian bobbed his head again.

Laurence stared at the frustrating man. "If, at any point, you do not know what to do, tell me. I will give you some advice."

"Very well."

One last time, Laurence studied Ian as if to triple check they were on the same page. He wasn't entirely convinced Ian knew what went on in a brothel. Ever since the elf joined Thessian's elite unit, he never showed interest in the opposite sex.

Does he prefer men? Laurence hugged himself and shuddered. *Surely not… He has seen me naked and never reacted.*

"Commander? What is wrong?" Sergey asked. "You have turned pale all of a sudden."

Laurence shook off the haunting possibility and joined the rest of the squad leaders with rejuvenated excitement.

"Come on, men! This will be a night to remember. I am certain of it."

Sergey took the lead while Laurence bantered with Eugene and Yeland.

Unlike Sergey, who resembled a true Hellion citizen with his sun-bleached blond hair, Eugene and Yeland had dark-brown hair and hailed from Darkgate. After the King of Darkgate was defeated and the land was consolidated with the Empire, Eugene and Yeland joined Prince Thessian's army.

The streets became darker and more ominous. A single lantern was lit in the middle of a grim, unnamed alley.

They waded through a muddy patch where the snow had recently melted. The wet dirt squelched under their boots.

In the distance, Laurence spied a cloaked figure.

The person gave four raps on the metal door, spoke to someone through the opened slit, and was permitted entry shortly after.

Laurence elbowed Eugene. "It is our turn."

He paraded towards the entrance and knocked four times.

A pair of unnaturally big eyes appeared on the other side of the slit.

In a tone so deep, it sounded as if it came from the bottom of a cavern, a man asked, "Passphrase?"

Eugene replied, "Iris."

The doorkeeper unlocked the door one lock at a time.

Laurence counted five locks before they could enter, and his gut twisted with uncertainty.

What kind of brothel requires such security? Are the women kept here against their will?

Finally able to see the doorkeeper in the dim light, Laurence barely contained his gasp.

It was no man.

What stood before him was a troll. Their kind were considered too stupid and violent to be kept around humans.

Upon closer inspection, he noticed a silver collar with a blood-red gem secured around the troll's neck.

That explains it—a control collar.

It was a pricey item sold by the Mage Assembly to subjugate monsters. Using it on humans or other humanoid races was illegal in the Empire. Whoever owned the brothel had to be swimming in gold to be able to afford such an expensive toy.

As Laurence was about to head inside, the troll raised its arm and produced another order, "No weapons!"

Laurence looked at his hip. He did not bother bringing his sword, only a dagger. He undid his belt and held the sheathed weapon in his hand. "Where can I put this in the meantime?"

The troll pointed to another door with a crudely made plaque that had 'Storage' carved into it.

Laurence dropped off his dagger, taking note that barely any weapons were in the so-called 'storage'.

Eugene, Yeland, and Sergey handed over their swords.

The rest of the squad leaders were smarter and did not bring any weapons.

Laurence assumed Ian had no weapons on him, as he did not move an inch.

"All done. Can we go in now?" Laurence asked the troll.

The troll grunted, "Mask."

Laurence spotted an array of clay masks hanging on the nearby wall. "Thank you, kind sir. Troll. Sir Troll?" He waved to the doorkeeper and picked out a mask with a fox painted on it.

Ian selected a wolf mask, and Sergey ended up with a rabbit as he was the last to choose.

Laurence peeled back the crimson curtain with a smile on his face. Finally, he was about to enter heaven and forget his troubles for the night.

Surrounded by luxurious fabrics, dozens of masked men waited for something.

A pleasant sound of a crystal harp calmed Laurence's nerves. He spied the harpist on a balcony above the cluster of patrons.

The eye-catching Elven maid had her eyes closed as she moved her slender fingers to stroke the fine strings.

"What do you think they are waiting for?" Sergey asked next to Laurence.

"Entry?"

Laurence assessed the other patrons. Their finely crafted boots and jewellery told him they were nobles or wealthy merchants. He was right all along. The brothel was for the elite. They truly stumbled upon a gem.

A man dressed as a butler, accompanied by white gloves and a ruby-studded mask, walked onto a stage under the harpist. He clapped his hands, drawing everyone's attention.

"Gentlemen, we have reached capacity early tonight. The entry will be permitted to you all momentarily while we prepare the merchandise."

Merchandise?

Laurence scowled behind his mask. Even ladies of the night deserved recognition as human beings. Although some customers preferred to only take pleasure from their women, Laurence enjoyed the game of give and take. Because of that, the ladies at The Golden Suns welcomed him with open arms.

The Ruby Mask noticed Laurence's group. In a cheerful tone, he said, "It appears we have new members among us! Do not be shy, gentlemen, and use the merchandise to your heart's content. We will calculate the fee based on the state of the merchandise after you have had your fill. For privacy reasons, please keep your masks on at all times."

What is he talking about?

The heavy feeling in Laurence's stomach returned.

Is this a brothel where the owner encourages violence? Surely no one in their right mind would wish for the women to suffer to the point of being unable to work. As for the fees…

Laurence only brought two gold coins with him. That was the average price for a night of pleasure in the Empire.

Will they ask for more?

He hoped the other squad leaders brought enough money to cover the expenses.

"…my assistants will soon ask if you have any special requests,"

The Ruby Mask continued with an unnerving chuckle. "Divulge all of your secret fantasies to us, and we will meet them."

Laurence peered at his men over his shoulder and noticed that they were not as disturbed by what they were hearing as he was.

Am I overreacting? After all, the nobility loved drama and embellished stories.

Laurence tuned out what The Ruby Mask was spouting when he saw how beautiful the assistants were. The ladies wore little, which had a part of his body getting ahead of itself. He scowled at the bulge in his trousers.

"My lord," a woman with honey-blonde hair, fair skin, and clear green eyes spoke to him in a melodic voice, "are there any special requests you would like to make?"

Laurence struggled to keep his eyes on her face. Behind her incredible beauty was the biggest, cushiest chest he had ever seen.

"Re-requests?" His voice came out as a squeak. He cleared his throat. "As long as I could have you all to myself, I have no other."

She giggled. "My lord is such a tease. Of course, it won't be us servicing you. The merchandise is much better than us, low-grade assistants."

His brows skyrocketed. *How could there be someone better?*

The Ruby Mask gestured towards another crimson curtain on his right after the quiet questioning of the last patron. "You may now enter your world of fantasy. Please enjoy yourselves, our dearest guests!"

Laurence itched to get to the other side. He did not seem to be the only one. The other men marched on beyond the curtain with much determination in their stride.

Laurence's turn came. He grinned as an assistant moved the curtain back for him. He followed a long, candle-lit corridor to a wide, central chamber where his smile faded faster than a falling star.

A long line of males and females no older than twenty stood gathered at the centre of the room. They were tied together with golden chains and a control necklace nestled on their necks. Aside from being starkly different from one another in appearance, none of them were human. Their eyes, unlike those of the hosts, were lifeless. Behind the slaves stood mercenaries with enough weapons to start an uprising.

Another assistant sashayed to him as if what he was seeing was normal. "My lord, would you like to choose your merchandise for tonight?"

He wanted to hurl.

Are these people blind?

Their *merchandise* did not seem happy to be there.

Laurence scanned the room for a corner, where he could get some privacy. "I think I will wait for my friends first."

The assistant gave him a knowing wink. "My lord enjoys company. I understand."

"What? Wait, I—"

"Have no fear. Your secrets will remain safe within our establishment. Not even the Lionhart Guild knows about our members."

Laurence dragged Ian and Sergey to one side as soon as they entered. Then he growled at Sergey, "Did you know this place would be full of enchanted slaves?"

Sergey's eyes were as wide as saucers. "No, sir! I had no idea! The merchant only spoke of girls being young and beautiful."

"Disgusting," Laurence hissed.

Ian fixed his gaze on the non-humans.

Laurence spotted an elf among them. The young man had a blank look in his eyes, the same as the others.

"Ian, believe me, I did not know," Laurence began.

His comrade did not seem phased. "What are your orders?"

Laurence blew out a heavy breath. He wanted to get away as fast as his legs could carry him, but that was no longer an option. The mercenaries were there to guard the merchandise and act as an imposing threat to the patrons to partake in the event. Once the deed was done, the establishment would have enough to blackmail the participants until their pockets ran dry.

He sensed from the establishment's members that they were not coerced or threatened. Some eagerly rubbed their hands before they touched their pick for the night.

Another attendant arrived at their side with a smile and a hint of impatience in her stride. "My lords, it is time to choose. Would you like to select one toy each or take one for all three of you?"

To keep up with the act, Laurence replied in a laid-back manner, "We are still deciding. You see, we have different preferences for our night partners, but we would all like to be in the same room."

She nodded. "Would you prefer to try different merchandise? We can offer as many as you'd like, for the right price, of course."

Laurence had never wished to punch someone as hard as The Ruby Mask and his vile assistants.

"I think I will choose one for us." Laurence looked at his men. "Are we in agreement?"

Sergey grunted, and Ian gave a curt nod.

"It is decided then," Laurence said triumphantly. "I will choose one."

The assistant led the way to the line of non-humans that had thinned out since his arrival. A lot of the older youths remained. He did not want to know what the younger prostitutes were going through.

Among the elves, half-orcs, halflings, and winged folk, one stood out—a red-headed beast-girl. Her wolf ears were pointed upwards, and the haze in her round silver eyes seemed to weaken.

Laurence could not believe a beastman existed in their day and age. They were supposed to be extinct a hundred years ago. Laurence once read they could live up to four hundred years old. Because of that, as with the elves, it was hard to gauge their age based on appearance.

Ian tapped Laurence on the shoulder and pointed to her. Although Laurence initially assumed Ian was staring at the elf next to the beast-girl, he was proven wrong.

"This toy may be too strong-willed for newcomers," the assistant warned. "It broke through the enchantment and attacked the clients on more than one occasion." She draped her arm over a female elf's shoulders and stroked the girl's ample breasts. "This one may be a better choice for you. She is obedient and takes punishment without a fight."

Laurence could not deny that on a normal day, he would choose the busty elf, but it was rare for Ian to make a request. If Ian was into beastmen, they had to pick her.

None of that had anything to do with the fact Laurence kept feeling guilty over fooling and dragging Ian along.

"As you can see, there are three of us," Laurence confidently told the assistant. "We will manage."

She smiled and separated from the Elven slave. "Very well. We are here to fulfil your fantasies, and should you choose to change merchandise for another, we will help you select a new one."

The assistant walked over to a mercenary behind the beast-girl and retrieved a glowing control crystal from him. She handed it to Laurence.

"Should the merchandise misbehave, please use this to subdue her."

Laurence accepted the crystal. "Thank you."

"Come this way, gentlemen." She beamed her perfect smile at them and led the way farther into the depths of the establishment.

Beyond an ornate door was a long corridor with many doors on each side. Each one had a golden number large enough to fill the entire door. Their establishment was flaunting their wealth left, right, and centre.

As they walked down the corridor, the only sound came from their boots and the banter of the assistant who was explaining the rules.

At the door numbered twenty-two, she stopped and detached a thick keyring from her hip. "You have one hour to do with the merchandise as you please. After the time is up, one of our male assistants will come to retrieve the merchandise and offer you the bill. If you wish to extend your stay, please inform him then."

Laurence looked from one door to another. "Why is it so quiet?"

"We use an enchantment of silence in these rooms. It was originally designed for great libraries, but we have repurposed it to suit our establishment's needs. As you can see, it will block all sound beyond the doorway."

"Clever."

"Thank you kindly for the praise." The assistant moved in front of a small painting on the wall and removed it. Behind it, she turned over an hourglass, allowing the grains of sand to speed to the opposite end.

She opened the door for them. "I hope you will enjoy your stay with us."

Laurence entered the room fit for royalty. He had never seen a bed as big as the one before him. It took up most of the space at the far wall. On the wall next to him, he saw a myriad of small torture devices neatly hanging on a rack.

What a disgusting place this is...

13

THE FLAMING ESCAPE

LAURENCE

Once Sergey, Ian, and the beast-girl were all in the designated room, the assistant shut the door, and Laurence heard the turn of the key.

They got locked in.

As there were no windows, he assumed the male assistants she talked about were the mercenaries who would beat the gold out of those who were unwilling or unable to pay.

"Sir Ian, give me your take on the layout." Laurence took a seat on the plush bed and removed his mask.

The others followed his example and took off theirs.

"The assistants in the first room came from the upper floor of the establishment, which shows there are other floors above us. Although there are no windows, we are on the ground floor and wedged between buildings. I have counted forty-seven mercenaries and ten female assistants, excluding the host in the jewelled mask and the troll."

"Wow! That is the most you have spoken in a year, I believe." Laurence glanced at the girl. "What do we do with her?"

"I should inform His Highness of her existence upon our escape," Sir Ian replied.

"I did not know His Highness was interested in their kind."

Ian returned to being tight-lipped.

Laurence narrowed his eyes. He knew His Highness got hurt during their trip to Count Fournier's territory.

Did they encounter a beastman?

It was possible. The wound Prince Thessian sported resembled an animal attack, and beastmen were known for their ability to change forms when in battle.

Sergey ran a hand over his face. "Commander, what are we going to do? The other squad leaders must be confused."

"If they saw how we behaved, they should be able to take a hint and act accordingly. I am positive Eugene and Yeland will figure things out on their own." Laurence rested his elbows on his knees. "Our main problem is, how do we get out of here in one piece? Any suggestions?"

"We could start a fire?" Sergey offered.

"We might burn to death before they take notice," Laurence commented. "Remember the silence enchantment?"

Sergey nodded grimly.

"Sir Ian, thoughts?"

"The door itself will produce sound if we bang on it, Commander. The enchantment spans to the doorway, not beyond. Judging by the attendant's words, this beast-girl is violent. They would not leave us in here without a safety net."

Laurence showed them the control crystal in his hand. "I believe *this* is the safety net." He ran his free hand through his hair and stared at the ceiling while he mulled over the possibilities. Banging on the door could work, but they had no weapons and nothing to start a fire with. "If only we had some weapons…"

"I have two daggers and five knives," Ian replied matter-of-factly.

Laurence's face lit up. "Of course you do!"

As there were four people in the room, and the space was quite limited, Laurence rose to his full height and started pacing around the bed.

"Our next problem is that we are greatly outnumbered." Laurence stopped mid-stride. "Sergey, what are the odds the other squad leaders did not hand over their weapons?"

"Quite low. They were expecting to come to a normal brothel."

Ian scowled at them. "I thought we were on a mission."

Laurence broke into an apologetic smile. "You see, Ian, this is a secret mission outside of His Highness' knowledge."

"You lied to me?"

"Not *lied*, per se. Amended the details a smidgen?"

Ian made his way to the door. "I will be returning to camp on my own."

"No! Wait." Laurence jumped over the bed and grasped Ian's shoulder. "I am sorry for lying to you. I wanted you to get friendlier with the others. You have been keeping a distance from everyone since you joined us. It is high time you learned to mingle."

Ian smacked Laurence's hand off his shoulder. "I did not join the unit to 'mingle'."

"I know. It won't happen again, I promise."

"Erm…Commander?" Sergey interjected. "The girl, she's— ACK!"

Laurence whipped around to find Sergey pinned to the floor by the beast-girl. Her hands had transformed into sharp claws and were about to dig into Sergey's throat.

Ian moved faster than Laurence could voice an order. He kicked her off Sergey and pointed his dagger at her.

She growled at them as her canines extended. The silver in her eyes looked molten in the lamplight.

After shaking off the initial shock, Laurence waved the control crystal in his hand. "Young lady, please be so kind and retract your claws. We are not here to hurt you."

She growled even louder. For a young girl, her body displayed more taut muscles than Laurence could ever dream of.

"*Vas ntes tietna, kaiedes i aunen!*" she snarled.

Laurence tilted his head to one side. "Does anyone here speak her language?"

Sergey scrambled to his feet. "This isn't the time for jests."

"*Im innas al-harna le,*" —*I will not wound thee*—Ian said each word in Elvish with great care. Gingerly, he removed his headscarf, revealing his pointed ears to the beast-girl. "*Im edhellen.*" —*I am of the Elves.*

She seemed confused as her eyes darted between them. "*Oin zaotuo yille eund dei arikeshe. Jya mopeca emberh vas.*"

A nervous smile froze on Laurence's face. "Do you think she understood you, Ian?"

Ian shrugged without taking his attention off the target.

"Great," Laurence grumbled.

Too bad Laurence's magnetism only worked on human ladies. He often had stray dogs chasing after him back home. They barked at him as if he stole their last bit of bone.

Unknowingly, Laurence clenched the control crystal in his hand, causing it to emanate a bright red light.

She spotted him and reluctantly retracted her claws. "*Jya werst vosie ointes, arikesh.*"

"I think she understood your warning, Commander," Sergey said.

"Even animals are afraid of pain. Since she is a beast, she will know what this crystal can do." Laurence raised his hands and took a slow step towards her. "How about it, girl? Will you be calm and let us figure out how to get out of here?"

She tilted her head to one side. "*Jya delte ankota. Osie kablenen fabise.*"

"Her desire to kill us has not dissipated," Ian informed them.

"We picked her because you told us to, Ian. Now, how can we plan our escape while keeping her in check?" Laurence tossed the crystal to Ian. "Deal with her while Sergey and I think things through."

Ian pointed to the wall and waved the crystal so she would see it. "Move there."

Narrowing her eyes, she made her way to where he pointed.

Ian motioned for her to sit, but she did not seem to understand the gesture.

She growled.

Laurence sighed and pulled Sergey to the opposite end of the room. His mind spun with the mess they ended up in.

I should have stayed in my tent and rested as His Highness ordered.

"What do we do?" Sergey asked.

"We cannot remain here for the full hour."

Laurence poured over the possibilities, all of which headed in the direction of letting the beast-girl loose on the mercenaries. They could attempt an escape during the commotion. The problem with that plan was the high chance she would die. For some reason, Ian seemed intent on bringing her back to Prince Thessian.

That plan is as good as useless.

"Ian, could you distract the guards while we find the others?" Laurence knew he was asking for a lot.

"I can."

"Good. Give the crystal to Sergey and unlock the door. We will have to split up. I will start a fire while Sergey locates the squad leaders and informs them of the plan."

Sergey raised his hands in the air. "I'm sorry, but I do not know how to use that thing."

"You hold it. Should she get out of hand, think 'obey'. At least, that is what a mage once told me," Laurence explained.

Sergey rubbed his sweaty palms against his trousers. He glanced at the girl, and she growled even louder. He jumped. "I do not think I will be of any use around her."

Laurence groaned. Sergey seemed terrified of her. Not that Laurence could blame him. He, too, was not keen on being around her. She was sure to attack the second they dropped their guards.

"Fine, I will take her with me," Laurence announced.

Ian handed over the crystal, along with two throwing knives. He gave one to Sergey and started for the door.

"Why do I only get one knife?" Sergey complained.

Laurence pointed to a wall of torture devices. "Help yourself if you are feeling low on weapons."

Sergey blanched. "I would rather fight with my bare fists than touch those."

Laurence replied, "Suit yourself. Among us, Ian has the most dangerous task. He cannot exactly go out there with a thumbscrew and some crocodile shears."

"Oh..."

Ian unlocked the door and peeked outside. "No one is in the corridor."

"Great. Sergey, Ian, go out first. I will start a fire."

Ian threw a small rock at Laurence, who nearly missed it.

Opening his palm, Laurence found a piece of flint there. "What don't you carry around with you?"

Ian smirked and secured his headscarf in place. He snuck out without making a sound.

Unlike the perfect example of stealth, Sergey stumbled over nothing in the doorway and apologised before running off.

Laurence closed the door behind them and faced his new companion. "I hope you understand we are in the same boat here."

She crossed her arms and upturned her nose.

They could not speak the same words, but body language may be enough. In case she tried anything, he gripped the crystal.

Laurence climbed onto the bed and cut the mattress open with a knife. Then, he pulled out a bunch of straw and sat on his haunches. He needed both hands to start a fire.

The crystal had to go.

Which would leave me defenceless.

Laurence eyed her with suspicion. She had not moved an inch. Her silver eyes, on the other hand, seemed to drill holes in his skull.

Why couldn't this be a normal brothel?

"Listen, I am going to get you out of here. To *safety*. Please *do not* attack me. Understood?"

She continued to stare at him.

Laurence cussed. "If only Sergey had taken you with him."

Slowly, he lowered the crystal onto the mattress but didn't let go. While he did so, she remained motionless.

He swallowed his nerves. *Maybe she understood me?*

The second the crystal parted with his skin; she lunged claws first. With unnatural speed, she toppled him and straddled his chest before he had a chance to blink.

Her sharp claws dug into his chest, where she gripped him by the coat.

Laurence coughed and gasped for air.

She wasn't just fast. Her strength was enough to crush his ribcage.

I guess she did not understand me, after all.

Mother, Father, I am sorry I did not get married to give you grandchildren.

She growled at him loud enough to make him wince. All thoughts of his goodbyes vanished. As she bent down, she sniffed him and frowned. Her nose kept getting closer until her face was buried in his neck.

Do beastmen bite off the necks of their victims?

Laurence shuddered. He wanted his body to return to the Empire in one piece rather than a bloody mess.

She made a strange noise Laurence could only assume was purring and rubbed her face against his cheek.

"We may be in a brothel, but I am not into underage girls."

She snarled in response.

Laurence gingerly held on to her shoulders and attempted to push her back.

Her claws dug deeper into his skin, making him stop. He lay back on the mattress and stared at the ceiling as he pondered his options. The others needed him to start a fire, as Ian would not make a good distraction for long.

Laurence inched his hands between their bodies and took hold of her furry paws. They were oddly soft. He peeled her hands back and used all of his strength to push her back a few inches.

"Please let go. I have to do something."

Her eyes bore into his until she sat upright. Long red tresses fell around her oval face and tickled his cheeks. Her thin lips parted and a set of pointed teeth looked back at him. *"Mir."*

"I swear, I do not taste all that goo—"

She bit his shoulder hard and drew blood.

Laurence felt around him for a knife. He touched the butt of the handle and got a hold of it.

As he was about to stab her, she jumped back and growled.

Sitting up, Laurence touched his bloody shoulder with his free hand. He hissed in pain.

"This is something the books about beastmen do not talk about."

Instead of attacking him again, she squatted near the bed, her mouth smeared with his blood. She grinned. This time, her teeth returned to normal and her claws retracted.

Laurence looked around for the control crystal. When he glanced back at her, he saw she was already holding it. She squeezed it in her palm, making it shatter into tiny pieces.

"There goes my safety net…"

Even then, she did not seem interested in killing him. She plopped down on the spot and waited.

After a minute-long staring contest, Laurence chanced starting a fire a second time. When she did nothing as he struck the flint against the dull side of the iron blade, he relaxed a notch and kept at it until the sparks lit the dry straw.

Soon, the mattress was burning like a bonfire during a harvest festival, and Laurence ran for the door.

The girl moved with him, not letting him out of her sight.

Laurence did not know whether to be thankful or worried as they burst into the corridor.

He looked left, then right.

The smoke reached his boots and kept gliding farther.

In the distance, he could hear mercenaries shouting orders at each other. That had to be Ian's doing.

"This way!" Laurence grasped her by the hand and pulled her along.

They came to a set of wooden stairs that led upwards. As there were no windows on the ground floor, he hoped there was at least one on the upper levels. He scaled the stairs as fast as his legs could carry him and listened out for any movement.

On the top floor, he heard footsteps rushing towards them. He pushed the girl into the first door on their left and quickly closed the door behind them.

The footsteps faded, and he heard a growl escaping from her.

Laurence jumped back. "I do apologise."

Looking around, he spied dozens of control crystals resting in glass cases. Bookcases lined the wood-panelled walls, with books written in a runic language used by the Mage Assembly. As tempting as it was to grab a crystal and resume control of her, he knew he would be dead before he could do so.

A few planks barricaded a single window that Laurence saw at the far end of the storage room. He ran towards it and yanked at the first plank. With the strain on his muscles, his wounded shoulder burned.

He pulled out a plank halfway before taking a breather.

The girl cautiously inched closer. She looked from him to the window. "*Wo sohen raci?*"

"What? Listen, we must get out through the—"

She dismantled the barricade with ease before he could utter the word "window".

Completely stumped, he muttered, "Good job?"

How did this establishment contain her all this time?

Laurence peered out of the window, finding a slanted roof of someone's house directly below. They could use that to escape.

He could see smoke rising from the lower floors and prayed the others got out unscathed.

Grasping the edges of the window frame, he started to climb out.

The beast-girl tugged on the sleeve of his coat.

When he peered over his shoulder, she was shaking.

Is she afraid of heights?

Laurence offered his hand. "Come. I will keep you safe."

He put on a cheerful smile, hoping the feeling in his words would reach her.

She tightened her grip on his sleeve and stepped forward.

Laurence lifted himself onto the ledge. While balancing on his haunches, he offered her his hand a second time. "Come here."

This time, she took his hand.

Without delay, he secured his hold on her and pushed them out of the window. Amidst their descent, he wrapped his body around hers to shield her from the harsh fall.

With a loud crash, followed by tiles and debris clattering all around them, Laurence landed on something soft. The landing may have been safe, but his body ached all over.

Once the ringing in his ears subsided, Laurence turned his head to find them lying on someone's bed. Not only that, the madam in question was screaming bloody murder.

Laurence grunted and pushed his body into a standing position.

He helped the beast-girl do the same.

"Hooligans! Mongrels! What are you doing in people's homes at night?" the madam screeched.

"I am so sorry for the mess. Send the bill to His Grace, Duke Malette. He will pay for the damages." Laurence saluted her and ran for the door before the rest of the household awakened.

14

WORDS OF A MAGE

EMILIA

Emilia had much to think about. Malette and Bishop Lagarde had consummated a rather devious plan to dethrone her.

Want to drive me to madness with nightmares? You'll pay for this!

She headed to the dungeon, which was near the tower she used to occupy.

Two knights on guard duty stood to attention when they saw her approaching and saluted her.

"Good evening, Your Majesty. How may we be of service?" a male knight on the left asked.

Emilia studied their features and complexions. They seemed to be native Dante folk and most likely worked for Count Baudelaire.

"I am here to see the mage. Let me through."

The guard on the right picked up a lantern. "It gets dark and cold in the dungeon when the sun goes down. Shall I find a servant to fetch you a warm coat?"

"No need. I won't be long."

The guard with the lantern nodded, and the other unlocked the metal door for them.

The guard led Emilia down a flight of stairs cloaked in thick, murky darkness. The light of a single candle in its glass case was nowhere near what she needed to see ahead.

She nearly slipped on a step. Centuries of use had filed the stone down, leaving it with a polished surface.

Flickering torches came into view at the bottom of the stairs, along with an invasive stench of human waste and mould.

She covered her mouth and nose with a handkerchief.

Although she was aware that dungeons were not meant to be accommodating, she couldn't take the chance of Duke Malette contracting an unknown illness before his trial. Changes had to be made to make the confinement more humane.

The emptiness of the cells began to feel oppressive as they walked farther in.

The guard stopped in front of metal bars and lit more torches around them before aiming the lantern inside the cell.

As darkness receded with the burning flames, Emilia noticed a skinny man kneeling on the stone ground. His gaunt face was marked with scars that went beyond his grey linen shirt. He had his hands and feet bound with shackles and an iron chain that connected to the stone wall.

"Is there a need to keep him restrained?" she asked.

"Lord Armel requested we do not untie him. According to him, this mage requires freedom of movement to weave nightmares. This should stop him."

Clayton certainly learned from his mistakes. "I want to speak with him. Open the door."

"Your Majesty, it is too dangerous. We are unaware of what he is capable of in his current state. Please, remain here."

She stepped closer to the bars and spoke in an authoritative voice. "Dream weaver, why did you wish to harm me and my kingdom?"

The mage craned his head and awkwardly leapt towards her.

A rattle of chains resonated throughout the dungeon. The bindings held tight, keeping the mage a safe distance away from the bars.

His greasy hair dangled in front of his slanted eyes in clumps. The dryness of his skin made her think he had consumed no liquids in days, despite hiding in the pantry.

"Cursed Queen, you are the one who will bring disaster to this land!" the dream weaver said in a hoarse voice.

She rolled her eyes. "Interesting. Tell me then, what gives you so much certainty about my role in the future that will plague this world?"

As far as I know, I should be rotting away in an unnamed grave somewhere.

"Great Luminos guided the vision of a high priest all those years ago. You are a calamity, a demon, a being that should not exist in this world. Under your feet, the skulls of babes and mothers will lay, sickness will thrive, and rivers will flow red with blood."

She had heard those words many times throughout her life. Without the princes and the king around, she hoped those rumours would fade into nothingness.

How wrong was I?

"The Church has quite a wild imagination. I must have missed the revised edition of the prophecy where they added dead babies," she replied with a laugh.

Her humour ran dry. "Why does a mage serve the Church?"

He ignored her and kept muttering to the floor. "I am a sinner who wishes to right his wrongs. Luminos brought down this curse upon me because worldly desires have tempted me! You should admit your sins and beg for forgiveness as you take your life, Cursed Queen."

"I am pleased the Church upgraded me from princess to queen. It sounds much more ominous."

She stepped away from the bars. The mage had been completely brainwashed. Any information coming out of him would be useless, as it was influenced by the dogmas propagated by the

Church of the Holy Light. Mercenaries would talk for the right price while a believer was indoctrinated to die a martyr.

When she turned to speak to the guard, the mage rattled his restraints and hollered, "Repent, demon! Repent and plead for forgiveness. While I am alive, no night for you will go without fright. No day shall pass without your suffering."

Emilia felt her eye twitch.

The Church and its followers wanted her to lose her mind. Too bad for them, she was in full control of her faculties. A few sleepless nights would not kill her while she got rid of her opposition.

"I am done here," she informed the guard. As an afterthought, she asked, "Where are the bishop and Duke Malette?"

"They are in their respective cells under strict guard on a lower level. Do you wish to see them?"

"No. That won't be necessary."

"Then please follow me out, Your Majesty."

Moments later, Emilia thanked the guards for their hard work and returned to the comforts of the palace and its bright corridors.

The Church's influence was hard to shake. Their fanatics were popping up to scare the citizens and hinder her formal coronation. First, they attacked her with the orphans, and now they were targeting her sanity by inflicting nightmares upon her.

Since their plans failed, what's their next move? Incite the townspeople to lynch me?

As chilling as that thought was, she could not rule out such a ploy.

If only I was reborn as a different character—a village girl or a noble's son. My life would be a thousand times easier.

Should I ask Thessian for his amulet again? The mage may be physically subdued, but what about his abilities? What if Clayton's theory is wrong?

Emilia balled her hands at her sides. She had to put some trust in her subordinates. Although Clayton was a recent addition to her team, he worked tirelessly to prove his loyalty.

Not like he can betray me. His curse prevents him from doing so.

In a long corridor on the first floor, she saw Ambrose talking to a maid who was biting her fingernails. She approached them with her head held high.

They quickly curtsied.

"What can I do for you, Your Majesty?" Ambrose asked.

"What is going on?"

"Galia is here to give me her usual report on the servants."

Emilia eyed the maid she had tricked into submission on the day of her family's funeral.

Galia Every appeared to have lost some weight. Her face had become slimmer and her arms thinner. The greatest change was in her fingernails. They looked as if she was gnawing on them for hours.

Emilia became interested. "I would like to hear this report."

Ambrose nudged Galia. "Speak, girl."

"Yes, Head Maid." Galia never once dared to lift her gaze. "T-the maids who were fiercely loyal to Lady Tamara Hester left the palace as per the head maid's instructions. Clara, a laundry maid, has been sneaking out at night to meet with a guard. I couldn't see his face well in the dark. I apologise."

"What are you so worried about that you would bite your fingers to the bone?" Emilia inquired.

Galia readily hid her hands behind her back. "I will wear gloves from now on. Forgive me, Your Majesty, for having you see such a dreadful sight."

"Her Majesty asked you a question!" Ambrose said sternly.

"There are g-ghost sightings, Your Majesty. Two maids and a guard have seen a man dressed in white walking down the corridors of the west wing. When they tried to approach him, h-he disappeared into thin air."

"A ghost?" People in Emilia's new world were quite superstitious. She had to remind herself that she was in a fantasy novel. Ghosts could be real.

Emilia peeked over her shoulder. *Surely not...*

"This tale is too absurd. I have personally investigated the scene and found nothing," Ambrose reported.

"The ghost comes at night when almost everyone is asleep!"

Galia protested.

"Did you see this ghost with your own eyes?" Emilia pressed.

The maid shook her head. "It was Nancy. We share a room. She went to fetch a jug of water before bed two nights ago. When she didn't return, I went looking for her. That was when I found her curled into a ball in the west wing. I have shared a room with her for almost a year. Nancy is not one to fib or play a prank."

Ghost or no ghost, Emilia's gut was telling her she should not let the matter go. This could be another trick from her enemies to spread mistrust among her servants and solidify the belief that she was, indeed, cursed.

"Ambrose, have Sir Rowell escort the guard and the maids who saw the ghost to my office. I want to hear their accounts. And bring a map of the palace."

"Yes, Your Majesty."

"As for you, Galia. Good job. Visit the physician and ask him to take care of your hands."

"You are too kind." Galia bowed low and scurried away.

Emilia asked, "What did you do to make the maids get in line so quickly?"

"Your Majesty taught me to treat others with kindness unless they are trying to kill us."

Emilia's lips tugged into a smile. "You were worried about the responsibility, but you seem to be excelling at the task I gave you."

"Lady Tamara Hester mistreated most of the maids, so they were more than happy to change sides when I mentioned the benefits under your rule. The ones who were loyal to her were fired to avoid trouble later."

"Yes, she had quite the temperament. Her kind act only extended to my father and the princes."

"Without Lady Hester's embezzling, I had more money to fill the gaps by hiring more maids. In this way, I managed to rearrange their working schedules to lessen their load and gave everybody two days off a month."

Emilia gave a nod of approval.

"There is a matter that requires your permission…"

"What is it?"

"On the former king's orders, Lady Hester punished any servants who were romantically involved with the guards. Galia told me that many maids were flogged and expelled for that reason. As you can see, the rule does not stop them from falling in love or having secret affairs. I believe it to be an unfair rule, especially because the guards never received equal punishment."

"Do what you will. You have free rein over the matters of the maids. And inform Sir Rowell of the rule change, so he can apply it to the male servants."

Ambrose nodded. "I have also received reports of the guards assaulting the maids in the past. As I have no sway over the guards, what would you have me do?"

"Good thing almost all of them died in the coup." Emilia balled her hands at her sides. "Should something like this happen again, have the Guard Captain give the culprit a good beating and expel them from the palace."

"As you command, Your Majesty."

Emilia half-joked, "Maybe I should have assigned you to be Guard Captain instead of Dame Cali."

Ambrose shook her head. "I am exactly where I belong, Your Majesty."

"I am pleased you enjoy your new position. Should you need anything, do not hesitate to inform me. I may be buried in paperwork, but I will always make time for those loyal to me."

Rose tinted Ambrose's cheeks. "It is my duty to share your burden, Your Majesty, not add to it."

"Would you like to share my paperwork, too?"

Ambrose shook her head. "I would not dare think I could fill your shoes, Your Majesty."

Emilia let out a laugh. "Even though they are two sizes smaller than yours?"

Ambrose laughed along.

"I am feeling much better after our talk," Emilia admitted.

"If it is your wish, I will even play the role of a jester. Although my sister often tells me my jests are not funny."

"Better not. It would ruin your image among the servants."
Taking on a more serious tone, Emilia added, "I will see you soon
in my office. We have a mystery to solve."

"I will make a fresh pot of rose tea for you."

Emilia had forgotten all about tea with what the mage said. At
least, with a worthy mystery to solve, she won't need to worry
about falling asleep tonight.

In her office, Emilia spread the blueprints of the palace across
her desk.

Two maids and a guard, who saw the ghost, alongside Sir
Rowell and Ambrose stood to attention.

Emilia sat in her seat. "Thank you, Sir Rowell, for gathering
everyone so promptly."

He inclined his head and smiled. "It was my pleasure, Your
Majesty."

She diverted her attention to the maids, who had their heads
hanging low. At random, she chose the chubby blonde with two
braids resting on her shoulders. "What is your name?"

When the maid didn't immediately answer, Ambrose pinched
the girl's arm.

The maid straightened up like a good soldier. "Nancy, Your
Majesty."

Emilia softened her tone to seem more approachable. "Nancy,
tell me about the ghost you saw."

The maid's complexion lost all colour as she fiddled with the
hem of her apron. "I-it was late at night. I was coming b-back to my
room from the k-kitchen when I saw a man dressed completely in
white. He-he—"

"Hold on." Emilia raised her hand. "Could you describe what
he was wearing?"

Nancy blinked several times. "'Twas a shirt and a long coat,

Your Majesty."

"Did you recognise him?"

The maid swung her head from side to side.

"What about his features? Was he tall, short, blond, dark-haired?"

"T-tall and fair-haired, with some patches of grey. A bit on the handsome side, Your Majesty."

The other maid nodded vigorously. "It's the same thing I saw!"

The guard joined in by giving a firm nod.

Emilia rubbed her chin in thought. The description reminded her of a man she once saw. She had only caught sight of him once on a night she was in the middle of sneaking out of the palace. At the time, she paid him no heed.

Could it have been Julio Grande?

Men from the central Hellion Empire often had blond or light-brown hair. The report Lionhart gave her said Julio was in his late forties. No doubt, he sported some grey hair. He had average height and average appearance for an Empire's citizen. And, most importantly, he smelled of arnica flowers.

"Did he smell of anything?" Emilia knew she was grasping at straws.

Nancy scratched her head. "He did smell of pine or sage."

"Like some medicine in Mister Benjamin's office," the second maid said.

Nancy and her colleague nodded to one another.

The guard shrugged. "I did not get a chance to sniff him."

The maids glared at him.

Emilia cleared her throat to bring the conversation back on track. "Tell me exactly where you saw him."

"The west wing's main corridor, on the way to the maid's quarters," Nancy replied.

Emilia marked it on the map with a pawn from her chess set.

The second maid's turn came. She appeared to be braver than Nancy. "I saw him lurking near the western tower. When I was talking to another maid 'bout it, a beautiful man came up to me and asked for more details."

Emilia furrowed her brows. There weren't many hunks at the palace. One of the individuals was Prince Thessian—an Adonis with blond hair. The next person was Clayton, who possessed the most dazzling eyes she had ever seen. She conjectured that Laurence could also be included, along with a groomed Lionhart.

Emilia recalled that Prince Thessian and Cali were the ones she met with on the day of the king's funeral. They were awfully interested in finding Julio.

Clayton, too, reported that Julio was originally sighted by his informant in the west wing's halls.

As she placed another pawn on the map, she put the scenario together in her mind.

One—the ghost is probably Julio Grande.

Two—Julio is somewhere on the palace grounds.

Three—he never left after King Gilebert died, which means whatever he's researching has to be at the palace. Maybe the item is impossible to move without anyone noticing?

What on earth did King Gilebert ask Julio to study?

"Guard, where did you see this ghost?" Emilia asked.

The soldier resembled one of the Hellion Empire's people. He had cloudy blue eyes and trimmed straw-coloured hair. He even spoke with a heavy accent. "It was in the west wing's corridor when I was doing my rounds. At first, I thought it was a person, so I gave chase. After turning the corner, I came to a dead end. That is when I realised what I saw could not be human, Your Majesty."

Emilia searched for a dead end on the map and asked the guard to verify the location.

He nodded, and she placed another pawn down.

"Thank you all," Emilia said with a pleased smile. "You are dismissed."

Sir Rowell ushered the guard and the maids out of the room, while Emilia studied the map.

"Only the west wing. Hmm…" She lifted her head. "Sir Rowell, are there any secret passageways in the west wing that are not on the original blueprints?"

"King Gilebert made several renovations to the west wing, Your

Majesty. I would not be surprised if he had intended for some escape routes to be built without the knowledge of the servants."

"Ambrose, bring me the map of the catacombs from the Royal Library. I want to check something."

Ambrose left the room in a hurry.

Emilia picked up her teacup. She inhaled the wonderful rose scent and felt a smile stretching her lips.

"You seem to be in a good mood," Sir Rowell commented.

"I just imagined the faces of two impulsive men who are desperately searching for someone and, here I am, an office worker almost, finding them by chance."

"I hope I am not one of those men, Your Majesty."

She beamed at her head butler. "You are the perfect example of a fine gentleman, Sir Rowell. I wish more men were as attentive as you."

His aged face reddened to his ears. "Your praise is too much for this old man."

"I give praise where it is due."

By the time she finished her second cup of tea, Ambrose returned with the map.

Emilia accepted the parchment and looked at the area beneath the west wing.

As I thought…

There was plenty of room for a secret passageway if the king installed a set of stairs somewhere. The highest chance of a hidden entrance was at the dead-end the guard mentioned. As the rest of the catacombs were not accessible from that area, unless a wall or two were destroyed, she had to identify an entry point.

"Sir Rowell, did my father leave behind an updated version of this map anywhere?"

"I am not aware of that," he replied apologetically.

King Gilebert had a lot more secrets than I'd anticipated.

All this time, she thought he was a mere side character who was corrupt to the core and acted as a stepping stone for Thessian's character development. Yet, seeing as the world around her was as real as her previous life, it made sense that the king had a secret or two. The absence of Julio's research in the king's documents did not prove that he wasn't conducting illegal experiments elsewhere.

"Ambrose, I want you to keep an eye on this area here." She pointed at the pawn marking the west wing's corridor. "Make it seem as natural as possible."

"Will do."

"And inform the maids who came here to not breathe a word about our discussion."

There was no need to keep the guard quiet. He belonged to Thessian's unit and, therefore, could not have been involved with Julio from the start.

The door to her office burst open, and Cali rushed in, panting as if she ran all the way here. "Your Majesty, we received a report that a huge fire broke out in the capital!"

"What?" Emilia frowned.

Are Malette's men creating another distraction?

Strange. She received a report from Lionhart that Malette's soldiers had retreated from the outskirts of Newburn. *Did they somehow sneak in instead?*

Thessian arrived in her office a moment later. "Your Majesty, we need to send additional men to put the fire out. I have already sent word to my encampment to do the same."

Emilia rolled up the map of the catacombs on her desk. "Dame Cali, send as many men as you can spare to deal with the fire, and double the guard on Duke Malette and Bishop Lagarde in case this is merely a diversion." She turned her attention back to the prince. "Your Highness, I have to ask you for a favour."

"What is it?"

"Please oversee this situation personally. It would not be a good idea for me to go there in person. The citizens still believe me to be cursed."

"Is there a contingency plan in case of a fire?" Thessian asked.

Emilia pursed her lips. "The former king did not pay much attention to the safety of his people, and I have not yet had the time to arrange such matters. Most of the locals will be working to quell the flames, and, thankfully, the people are not as incompetent as they are superstitious."

Thessian was silent for a brief moment. "Very well. I will resolve this matter in your stead."

"Sir Rowell," Emilia called, "have the servants open up the stores and arrange for blankets and food to be prepared for those displaced. Please use the castle's outer ground as it is mostly empty grass."

Sir Rowell inclined his head. "I will arrange everything at once."

"Ambrose, you know what to do."

Everyone left her office in a hurry.

Emilia blew out a heavy breath and walked to the window. The moon glowed in the sky and black smoke in the distance rose to meet it. The market chapel's bells began ringing in alarm over her racing heartbeat.

Do I really bring catastrophe?

15

THE GREAT FIRE

LAURENCE

Laurence held on to the hand of the beast-girl and ran as far from the brothel as his legs could carry him.

Out of breath, he bent over and gasped for air.

"What a mess! I cannot believe we got away."

He faced the girl who had taken a few steps back. The trust she displayed earlier was gone, only to be replaced with weariness.

Laurence cautiously raised his hands. "I do not plan on hurting you. You can relax."

He smiled, hoping to convey his harmlessness.

She fired back with, "*Jya ne fera werst vosie hedu, arikesh.*"

"Will you come with me to the palace? We will help you."

She growled and broke into a sprint away from him.

Laurence cursed as he chased after her. His lungs and muscles burned from overworking that day.

When he turned the corner, she was gone.

"What terrible luck? Today is not my day."

His ears picked up the loud ringing of the warning bells throughout the city. He whipped around, and his jaw nearly came undone. In the direction of where he came from, the night sky had turned a mixture of red and orange hues. "No… It cannot possibly be because of that small fire."

He scanned the area for the last time, hoping to catch the elusive beast-girl.

Laurence raked his fingers through his hair.

How am I going to explain this mess to His Highness? He let out an exasperated sigh.

I will think about that later. First, I need to find the others.

He headed towards the commotion.

People were running out of their homes with their belongings cradled in their arms. Many of the residents scrambled to put out the roaring fire that ate away the sides of the tightly-knit houses and storefronts. Shivering children huddled next to their mothers — most underdressed for the cold.

A crowd of men had formed on the street. In no time, they were organized and running back and forth with buckets.

Surely, the fire will be put out soon.

A tap on his shoulder made Laurence jump. His eyes grew wide when he saw Prince Thessian there with Dame Cali.

Over fifty soldiers stood in a formation behind them.

"What are you doing here, Laurence?" Thessian raised his hand before his subordinate could reply. "I will get the answer out of you later. Right now, we must deal with this crisis. Cali, divide the men into three groups. Have two groups tear down the buildings in advance to stop the spread of the fire. They may use any means necessary. The rest should focus on helping the citizens while the fire brigade takes care of the rest."

Cali saluted him. "At once, Your Highness."

Laurence followed Thessian to a group of over thirty able men who threw water at the side of a three-storey building on Market Street.

"Who is in charge here?" Thessian demanded.

An older gentleman, dressed in fine clothes that must have cost a fortune, split away from those gathered.

"I am," the nobleman replied.

"I am here on orders from Queen Emilia. She sent the royal guard to help with the fire," Thessian informed the man.

"Good. There can never be too many helping hands." The noble ushered them to one side, away from the busy crowd. "I am Count Edmund Baudelaire. If I recall correctly, you must be Prince Thessian of the Hellion Empire."

"You know me?" Thessian asked with an edge to his voice.

"I have a flourishing trade relationship with Prince Cain, and you resemble him and His Imperial Majesty quite a lot." The pleasantness faded from Lord Baudelaire's tone. "Her Majesty may have a deal with you, but I do not. Our faction does not support the rule of a bloodthirsty warmonger. I suggest you take your men and leave Newburn."

"Regardless of what you may think of me," Thessian countered, "I came here at Emilia's request."

"I will cooperate if it is Her Majesty's desire." Lord Baudelaire's lips stretched into a wicked smirk. "I hope you know how to use a bucket, Your Imperial Highness."

The night ended, making room for the rising sun that ultimately displayed the damage Laurence had caused to the city. He remained silent as he continued to work alongside His Highness by passing buckets of water back and forth.

Forget painful. He was on the verge of collapsing due to overworked muscles.

The prince must have noticed something was amiss and pulled Laurence out of the long chain of people.

"You are too quiet, Laurence. You must be exhausted."

Laurence was in no mood for jokes. He glanced around him, taking in the terrible sight of the charred and destroyed homes. The blaze had consumed a part of a district. Had the prince not ordered the soldiers to isolate the fire, it may have engulfed the entirety of Newburn.

His shoulders slumped. He was at fault and had yet to see Ian or the other squad leaders.

Did they make it out alive?

He shuddered at the possibility that they could have been burned alive along with the brothel.

Prince Thessian placed a hand on Laurence's shoulder. "What is the matter with you?"

"Your Highness, there is something I need to confess. The fire—"

"Commander? Is that you?" Sergey ran over to them, along with Yeland and Eugene. They appeared to be unharmed. "We are so glad you made it out of there!"

Thessian faced the squad leaders. "Out of where?"

Sergey and the others stood to attention.

"Y-you were h-here, sir?" Sergey stumbled over his words.

"Why are my squad leaders in the city?" Thessian snapped.

Sergey glanced nervously at Laurence, who sighed.

"Your Highness, let them go." Laurence hung his head low. "I will explain everything."

"Help put the fire out, men!" Thessian waited until they were out of earshot. "What is this about, Laurence?"

Laurence could not meet His Highness' eyes. "We came here for a bit of fun. What we thought was a normal brothel ended up being an underground den for nobles who used control crystals on non-humans. We discovered a beast-girl there, and Sir Ian insisted we bring her to you. Amidst our escape, I set fire to the building and—"

"Tell me this is not your doing!"

Laurence's head snapped up. That was the first time he heard Prince Thessian's voice trembling with such anger. Not once had the enemies of the battlefield or their leaders gained such animosity from His Highness.

The prince's face, although smeared with dirt and grime, reddened.

Laurence lowered his gaze. "I am so sorry."

A second later, Thessian's fist collided with Laurence's jaw.

The sudden burst of pain across Laurence's face could not amount even to a smidgen of shame he felt. Thinking on it, the prince must have held back because Laurence's jaw did not get dislocated on impact.

Other than apologising endlessly, Laurence did not know what to do. He kept his head down while his eyes stung with tears. As Thessian's second-in-command, he had failed his superior.

"Who else is involved in this?" Thessian growled.

Laurence fell onto his knees. "I was the one who gave the order, so I will take full responsibility!"

"Do not make me repeat myself."

Defeated, Laurence eventually replied, "I came here with the squad leaders and Ian."

"Ian is here?" The prince went silent for a minute.

Laurence did not dare lift his head.

"Did he come here willingly?"

"No. I coerced him into believing it was a mission given by you."

"That makes more sense. Where is the beast-girl you mentioned?"

Laurence grimaced. "She escaped."

"Other than this disaster, there is nothing for you to show me, Laurence. I am disappointed in you." Thessian's voice was colder than the morning chill that bit into Laurence's skin. "As of this moment, you are relieved of your position. You and those involved will pack your belongings and return to Darkgate to await your punishment."

Laurence balled his hands in his lap. "Please, Your Highness, give me a chance to redeem myself. I will do anything!" He raised his head, unable to hold back his tears. "Give me one last chance!"

Prince Thessian appeared like a mountain, casting a vast shadow over Laurence's shrinking form. "You have one hour to find the others while I consider your punishment."

"I-I understand."

Thessian stormed away to speak to Lord Baudelaire as Laurence climbed to his unsteady feet. He wiped his face with the sleeve of his shirt to hide his tears. Since their arrival in the Dante Kingdom, nothing had gone right.

He massaged his aching jaw.

No. Dante has nothing to do with it. Everything is my fault for being an idiot.

Laurence ran around the city, searching for the squad leaders and Ian. Yeland and Eugene informed him that the others were helping put the fire out, so the remaining squad leaders were easy to locate. Sir Ian was nowhere in sight.

Laurence searched the crowds, the shelter, and the food distribution area for the wounded.

Ian was not there.

As a last resort, and with great trepidation, he checked the carts with the dead bodies. The charred remains were hard to tell apart.

Laurence whispered a prayer for their souls to find peace in the afterlife.

A chilling thought made his stomach sink. The brothel burned to the ground, leaving rubble behind. It was unlikely anyone trapped in the blaze would be recovered.

Laurence voiced his thoughts out loud, "Don't tell me Ian is dead."

"Who is dead?" the elf asked from behind Laurence.

Laurence spun around so fast, it took a moment for him to gather his bearings. "Ian? Is that truly you? You did not die?"

"No, Commander. I managed to escape."

Laurence's happiness dwindled when he saw multiple lacerations and bruises all over Ian's body. "You need treatment immediately."

Ian shrugged one shoulder and winced. "Do not worry about me. Elves heal faster than humans."

"That is not the point!" Laurence groaned. What he was about to ask Ian would delay his treatment. "Will you come with me to see His Highness?"

Ian nodded.

"I will tend to your wounds right after we see him."

"No need, Commander."

"Stop. I am not your commanding officer anymore." Laurence swallowed the knot forming in his throat. He was a mere soldier now. "I was stripped of my rank."

Ian said nothing. Not even a word of encouragement.

"I will lead you to His Highness."

16

ASHES AND DUST

THESSIAN

Thessian **wiped the sweat off his brow.** The fire was finally under control, but at a great cost. Half of the street was irreparable once the flames were finally put out.

The men who took part in putting out the flames appeared exhausted under a mask of dirt and grime stuck on their faces.

One of Lord Baudelaire's knights approached Thessian with a jug of water. "My Lord sends his regards and wishes to speak with you in private."

Thessian gulped down the water. The cool liquid felt like heaven as it soothed his parched throat. He returned the jug and wiped his mouth with the back of his sleeve.

"Lead the way."

The knight inclined his head and strode towards the tent erected for those who had lost their homes to the fire.

Inside the tent, Lord Baudelaire helped bandage the burn victims. Unlike most nobles who would not bother sparing a thought for those below their station, Lord Baudelaire did not shy away from the horrid situation. Throughout the night, Thessian could tell that Edmund Baudelaire did not help others for something in return. He genuinely cared about the lives of others and their suffering. Such a fine noble was hard to come by. It was unfortunate that Thessian did not have Baudelaire on his side.

If he is on Emilia's side, he is on my side now. She seems to be a better judge of character than I have anticipated.

Thessian approached him. "Do you require any help?"

Lord Baudelaire finished dressing the wound and thanked the old woman for her patience.

The woman patted the nobleman's hands with a grimy hand. "Thank you, milord, for helping this old crone."

The lord smiled kindly. "I should thank you for allowing me to practice my bandaging skills."

She laughed. "You are too kind! May Luminos guide you."

Lord Baudelaire looked at Thessian. "Please come with me."

They reached a quiet corner of the tent, separated from the rest with a thick grey curtain. There were no seats, only some barrels and crates, which Thessian assumed were the items salvaged from the storehouses.

With a sweeping bow, Lord Baudelaire said, "On behalf of the citizens of this kingdom, I would like to thank Your Highness for helping us. I heard it was because of your orders that the fire was managed so well. Your actions have saved countless lives and livelihoods."

Thessian rubbed the back of his neck. "There is no need for such formalities."

"I can see why Her Majesty chose to side with you. I will provide her with a detailed report on the situation and your contributions."

"A reward wasn't my motive for coming to help. I have plenty of achievements in my name in the Empire."

"Yes. You do." Lord Baudelaire mulled over his next words for a long minute. "I apologise for offending you. Your character surprised me. It is not as the rumours say."

"I am a proponent of judging people's character by their actions, not idle chatter. I pray Lord Baudelaire would do the same in the future."

The old noble cracked a smile. "Nobility relies on reputation to survive. Although Your Highness may have a reputation as a hero in the Hellion Empire, you are a looming threat in Dante. I implore you to leave as soon as possible. If you stay longer, it may negatively impact how other nobles perceive Her Majesty. There are even whispers that she is a puppet queen, and such rumours cannot lead to anything good."

Thessian intently studied the man.

Lord Baudelaire genuinely appeared concerned for Emilia's safety. Those rumours about her, despite being partially true, had to be squashed.

"I will consider your suggestion once I resolve a personal matter."

"I pray your personal business will be concluded here soon."

Thessian left the tent while deep in thought. The longer he stayed near Emilia, the more nobles would recognise him. Yet, leaving a young lady to manage a kingdom made him nervous. He trusted her enough to take care of her people, but not enough to not betray him.

Emilia claimed she was on his side. Ultimately, all he had was her word.

She sacrificed her family for survival. How trustworthy is an individual like that?

He rested his back against the side wall of a nearby building and rubbed his tired eyes. Unlike the other women in his life, Emilia bypassed his defences in less than a month.

Is it because she can see the future?

Probably not.

She felt comfortable to be around, like an old friend who knew him better than anyone else. Instead of being cautious and on alert, all he managed was a sliver of distrust.

She is a dangerous woman.

"Your Highness, is this...where you...were?" Laurence spoke between gasps. "I have been searching...everywhere for you!"

Thessian's moment of peace ended too soon. He pushed away from the wall.

The squad leaders of his advance forces and Ian stood behind Laurence's back. Punishment of his men was unavoidable as the consequences of their actions brought disaster upon Newburn.

"Is this everyone involved?" Thessian asked.

Laurence hung his head. "Yes, Your Highness. Please allow the others to return to camp. I will take full responsibility."

"You can't!" Sergey pushed past Laurence. He slapped his hand to his chest and half-shouted, "It was me who suggested the outing! Punish me instead!"

The other squad leaders nodded to each other and joined in, each claiming responsibility for their actions.

Thessian raised his hand to half the assault on his eardrums. "Enough! Look around you. None of you are without fault."

They lowered their heads in shame.

"Ian, tell me your side of the story."

Ian glanced at Laurence and sighed.

In a deadpan voice, the elf replied, "We entered the brothel for some fun and discovered that its 'attendants' were non-human slaves whom were being tortured and imbued with illegal magic to enforce their obedience."

Ian's tone became more engaged as he added, "Furthermore, we encountered a beast-girl, who may know the location of their tribe. We decided to exit the property with haste instead of participating while attempting to rescue the beast-girl. Amidst our escape, Laurence was tasked with starting a small fire to create a diversion. It appears, the slavers did not attempt to extinguish the fire, and, according to reports from the squad leaders, have used it to destroy evidence and dispose of bodies before fleeing the premises. We assume that they are wanted individuals and did not want to get questioned. This, unfortunately, left the slaves who were unable or unwilling to escape inside to die."

Thessian eyed the squad leaders who did not dare raise their heads and returned his attention to Ian. "Do you believe the beast-girl might belong to the Grey Wolf's tribe?"

"Yes, Your Highness," Ian replied matter-of-factly.

"Did you try to communicate with her?"

"It was a failure."

Thessian sighed. "Was she stronger than you?"

"Yes."

There was no doubt in Thessian's mind his men would have suffered losses if they encountered a beastman as strong as the Grey Wolf.

Maintaining a stern tone, Thessian said, "You are all dismissed from your positions as of this moment. Return to camp and pack your belongings. You will be returning to Darkgate where Ludwig will put you to work."

"May I make a suggestion?" Ian asked.

"Go on."

"Please allow Sir Laurence and I to track her down."

Thessian rubbed his chin in thought. "Do you believe she could be an asset?"

"That would be for you to decide."

Taking a closer look at Ian, Thessian saw a multitude of lacerations all over the elf's battered body. Ian needed treatment before his wounds got infected. Since he was the least guilty member of the team, listening to his request was not a bad idea.

"Very well," Thessian finally replied. "Find her and see if there are more of her kind. If there is a hidden village somewhere, we need to be aware of its existence and the threat it could pose."

Sergey joined the conversation. "Allow me to go, too. It would be dangerous for them to go alone."

"We also agree," the other men chimed in.

At least, they are willing to work as a unit.

"Once Ian's injuries have healed, I will consider who will go," Thessian said.

The men nodded grimly.

Laurence was oddly quiet.

"Ian, head to the palace to get treated. Laurence, stay behind.

The rest of you, return to camp."

The men dispersed, leaving the two of them alone.

"I know you regret your decision, Laurence. I want you to do your best to keep our men alive on this mission. Beastmen are formidable foes."

"Your Highness—" A shine of determination returned to Laurence's dull eyes, "—I will bring them back safely."

"And no more brothels."

Laurence wiped at the corner of his eye. "That, I cannot promise."

17

BITTER

LAURENCE

Laurence paced the length of the infirmary after his shoulder was dressed and bandaged.

The physician was taking his time looking at Ian's wounds.

One glance at Ian's body provided all the information Laurence needed. Ian's injuries were on the light side except for the bleeding sword wound on his back.

As the physician cauterised the wound, Ian bit into a cotton cloth and kept his eyes squeezed shut.

"There are no major problems," the physician announced when he dressed the wound. "Change the bandages frequently and avoid getting water on the wound for a week. You are in luck. Elf physiology will help your body heal quickly."

Ian removed the gag and nodded.

The physician glanced at Laurence. "If there is nothing else, I must tend to other patients."

"Thank you," Laurence replied.

The physician shuffled away.

Laurence sat on the now-empty stool next to Ian's bed. "How are you feeling?"

"I am fine, Commander."

Laurence grimaced. "I am no longer your commanding officer. Just call me Laurence." Knitting together his fingers in his lap, he swallowed his nerves. "Listen, I apologise for deceiving you. Because of me, you got hurt and could have died." When Ian did not respond, Laurence hung his head. "I mean it. Once you are all better, you can punch me."

"That won't be necessary."

"Are you sure?" Laurence rubbed his jaw unconsciously. "I am willing to sacrifice my handsome face for you."

"We put a temporary stop to a disgusting place. There is no need for apologies. I believe His Highness also knows this."

"He may never forgive me for this mistake…"

"We should focus on locating the girl."

Laurence gave a curt nod. "You are right."

Cali burst into the infirmary with her complexion as pale as the elf's. "I heard what happened. Commander, Sir Ian, are you badly hurt?"

Laurence waved his hands in front of him. "I am perfectly fine, but Ian got hurt because of—"

"I was careless," Ian interjected. "Dame Cali, congratulations on your new appointment."

She pouted. "I do not care about that."

Laurence managed a crooked smile. "You have to stay by His Highness' side and protect him. Do not make the same mistake as me."

Laurence's bitterness came out despite his attempt to hide it. He got up and patted Ian's shoulder. "I will find us something to eat."

"I will join you, Commander." Cali chased after him.

Laurence heard her hurried steps behind him and stopped in the hallway. He turned on the spot, making her bump into his chest.

Grasping her by the arms, he peeled her away from him.

"*Commander* Calithea Louberte, please leave me alone."

"Sir Laurence, I—"

"You have my sincere felicitations on becoming the unit's commander. You deserve it."

His hands formed fists at his sides, and he marched away when she looked ready to cry.

Calithea Louberte was a wonderful, hard-working woman. He did not deserve someone like her. The years he spent training her in swordsmanship were past them, as was the closeness they shared as teacher and apprentice.

In the military, rank reflected responsibility a person shouldered. Laurence could not make a move on her or return her feelings as her direct superior. So, he decided to marry whomever his parents chose.

The Oswalds were a powerful noble family because they made good connections through marriage. Love was not on the table. To support Thessian's pursuit of the Empire's throne, Laurence had to do all he could to attain more political power.

Now more than ever.

Should I write Mother? She is bound to have marriage candidates lined up.

Cali and I will move on once I am engaged.

He rested his back against the wall and hit his head against it. "She will be just fine without me."

18

FRIEND AND MENTOR

EMILIA

As the rays of the morning sun filled Emilia's office, she let out a loud yawn. Thankfully, no one was there to comment on her lack of manners.

Not that they would dare.

Emilia stretched and peeled her posterior away from her cushy chair. A night full of reports on the fire's spread and its eventual containment kept her busy.

With one glance out of the window, she could tell the fire was on its last embers. She had to think of a way to reward the palace staff for their hard work. Perhaps some time off would do wonders for morale.

A knock on the door alerted her.

Her guard came in and announced, "Mister Lionhart is here to see you, Your Majesty."

I guess he didn't get any sleep, either.

"Let him in. Send word to the kitchen to have breakfast served in the dining room."

"Yes, Your Majesty." The guard ducked out of the room.

Emilia wondered who he belonged to. His accent was from the southern region of Dante, yet most of the Baudelaire soldiers had a western accent.

Lionhart strode in with his limp more pronounced than usual and closed the door behind him. "Rough night?"

She smiled. "You look no better with the crescent moons under your eyes."

"I came to inform you that the fire was successfully put out. There were some casualties, but Count Baudelaire and the palace guards you've dispatched kept them to a bare minimum."

"That is wonderful news." She stayed away from any form of seating, as she may fall asleep at any moment. "Would you like to take a stroll in the garden before the food is served?"

"I need to stretch my legs, otherwise I am going to gain too much weight from sitting around all day."

"I heard you spent your time lounging around or sleeping in the afternoons at the guild."

He cleared his throat. "Those are baseless rumours."

"Of course." She tapped her chin with her index finger. "If I recall correctly, it was Sally who told me about it. She is not the sort to lie."

Lionhart cleared his throat. "I did my fair share of work."

She laughed, feeling the tension from the night's events dissipating. "I am sure you did. Well then, shall we?"

On her way to the door, she paused. "The guard outside my door, is he one of your people?"

He smirked. "I am pleased you noticed. His name is Antonio. He used to work for the guild. It is thanks to him we have as much information on Duke Malette as we do. He is skilled in combat and information gathering. Feel free to use him."

"Is he reliable?"

"His family is poor. Working for me helped him pay for his

mother's medicine. I believe he joined the guild out of gratitude."

"People in poverty are easily bought."

"Anyone can be bought as long as the price matches their needs."

That wasn't news to her. The corrupt nobles had enjoyed their frivolous lifestyles for too long in Dante.

She led the way to the inner courtyard, where she sucked in a long breath of fresh air. What spoiled her view were the ugly statues King Gilebert had commissioned. Every time, they made her eye twitch.

"I should get rid of those things," she muttered to herself.

"This is your palace. Do as you like."

She smiled. "I will have Sir Rowell put them on auction. The gold can replenish the empty palace coffers."

"This kingdom is lucky to have such a frugal queen."

"Do you recommend following my father's example when it comes to spending?"

They headed towards the fountain at the centre of the garden.

"You are perfect as you are, Emilia. After the things you have been through, you deserve to be happy. I will help you achieve your dream, whatever it may be."

"Have you accidentally stumbled upon a book of poetry somewhere?"

"I mean it. As your friend and mentor, I will stand by you."

Emilia wished someone like Lionhart could have been her father instead of Gilebert. Her two lifetimes were filled with bitterness and anger. She fought hard to keep her composure, but she couldn't hold back the stray tears that escaped.

He offered her a linen handkerchief and looked at the clear skies. "It must be raining."

"Indeed." She dabbed at her eyes. With her composure restored, she asked, "Since when do you carry handkerchiefs around?"

Lionhart made a sour expression. "To work in the palace, I must mimic the nobles."

"Has anyone mistreated you?"

"Even if they tried, I know all of their dirty laundry. They will only end up insulting themselves."

Emilia's respect for Lionhart rose. He could blend in anywhere and become anyone. She was right to ask him to become her spymaster. The role suited him perfectly.

At the fountain, she wrapped her arms around her middle. The morning air was as chilly as ever.

Lionhart stripped out of his coat and wordlessly draped it over her shivering shoulders.

She could have pushed his kindness away, yet she didn't. He had given up his freedom as guild master to be tied to the palace with her. To a man who hated dealing with nobles and royalty, palace life was possibly the same as a noose around his neck.

"Have you unearthed anything else from questioning the prisoners?"

"Duke Malette insists he was wronged," Lionhart said, slipping his hands into his trousers' pockets. "As for the bishop, he cracked faster than I could take out my toolkit."

She raised a brow. "Did you torture them?"

"No. As tempting as it was, I merely used it as a scare tactic."

"What did the bishop say?"

Lionhart lowered his voice. "Some of the Church's cardinals are against you being on the throne. If you bring prosperity to this kingdom, it will shake the foundation they had built with their prophecies. For the Church to succeed, you must fail."

"Do you think they started the fire in the capital?"

"I have planted some eyes around the temple. No one reported any priests leaving the premises before the fire. That does not mean there are no secret passageways…"

"Look into this matter for me. If the Church is behind this tragedy, the citizens must know which temple to burn. It will give me a chance to lessen the grip the Church of the Holy Light has on this land."

"I will make some enquiries." Lionhart watched the way the fountain tirelessly spewed water from the three jugs the naked female statues sported on their shoulders. "Do you plan to sell this work of art?"

"Why? Want to keep it? Should I have it moved to the small patch of grass near the tower?"

He shuddered. "I'd rather avoid such embarrassment, or Sally will never let me live it down."

Emilia giggled.

They circled the fountain and headed back towards the palace.

"Regarding the position of Guard Captain, I would like to make a suggestion."

"Oh?" Emilia was all ears. She did not want to keep Dame Cali there long enough to sprout roots.

"How about reinstating Jehan in the military? He had earned a lot of respect and achievements before your brothers forced him out."

Emilia pursed her lips. Her brothers did yet another dumb thing while they were alive. Highly likely, the list of their misdeeds had no end.

"Tell me more about Jehan. I have met him at the guild, but we never spoke for more than two minutes."

"He is one of the guild's founders. Seven years ago, when Jehan lost his position as a vice general of the king's army, his wife could not stand their new lifestyle and left him. He ended up living on the streets, which is where we first met."

"I may need to apologise to him on behalf of my deceased brothers. I am positive they must have shifted the blame to Jehan to appease the king's anger." She looked up at him. "Do you think Jehan will accept the position?"

"I have seen him polishing his old military sword many a time. He will always be a servant of the kingdom to his last breath."

"Very well. Send him a summons to the palace."

"I will let him know."

They came to a stop outside of the double doors that led back to the palace halls.

Emilia shrugged off his coat and handed it back to him. "I hope a day will come when you will tell me how an assassin became a leader of an information guild."

He smirked. "We have had such a pleasant conversation today,

Your Majesty. Why ruin the mood with old and forgotten tales?"

She sensed he put up his defences the second he mentioned her title and pried no further.

"Are you not going to have a meal with me?"

He bowed. "I have matters to attend to."

"Thank you for your company this morning, Lionhart."

Emilia strode into the palace without looking back. When he used her title, it felt like a mockery of her position.

You're overthinking. He probably suffered a lot and doesn't trust others easily. You are no different.

In the end, absolute trust is a road paved to Hell together.

19

BAD HOBBIES

EMILIA

Emilia finished her breakfast in the dining room and sluggishly retreated to her bedchambers for a bath.

The palace was unnaturally quiet, so the clicking of her low heels echoed down the hall.

While most of the servants were aiding the townspeople after the fire, she couldn't shake the unsettling feeling around her. It reminded her too much of her tower.

She hugged her sides and shuddered. *Memories like that are best forgotten.*

Ha! Easier said than done…

She arrived in her room and closed the door behind her. As she walked to the bathroom, she stripped out of her tight dress, letting it fall to her feet. She stepped out of the circle of soft material and started undoing the bow of her chemise when she sensed someone watching her.

She launched for her bed and pulled out a dagger from under her pillow.

"Come out at once!"

Her balcony doors opened, and Clayton glided in with his hands raised. He wore a navy coat embroidered with silver thread over a white shirt and a pair of black trousers that matched the colour of his leather boots. As usual, his hair seemed to be perfect, although he had climbed the side of the castle.

"Greetings, Your Majesty."

She narrowed her eyes, making him falter. "Is it your hobby to spy on undressing ladies, Lord Armel?"

He bowed low. "I apologise. I wanted to come in sooner, but you had taken off your clothes before I had the chance."

Emilia blushed and studied her cotton knee-length chemise. Her clothes were not see-through, but she felt naked under his burning gaze.

"Turn around, Clayton. It is rude to stare."

He complied, and she grabbed a cloak from her closet and draped it over her shoulders.

Taking a seat on the bed, Emilia slid her dagger under her pillow and crossed her arms.

"You can turn around. Did you come here to tell me you have found Julio?"

Clayton faced her and stood to attention. "Not yet. I came to report on a different matter."

"What is it?"

"Duke Malette's son has put out a request for your head."

Emilia nearly burst out laughing.

How many people wanted her dead? The corrupt nobles, Duke Malette and his allies, the Church of the Holy Light, and God knows who else? Acting as regent was looking like an empty grave with her name on the headstone. Yet, she could not allow Prince Kyros to claim the Empire's crown. He would destroy the continent with his conquests to slaughter the mages and their allies.

She asked, "Did House Escariot receive this mission last night?"

"Yes. We have yet to respond. Would you like for us to eliminate the Duke's family?"

"Not yet." Killing them off was easy, and she was sure Duke Malette had his fair share of enemies. The problem was that the people in his territory liked him more than they hated him. They might take up arms against her with great vigour if they suspect her involvement.

After much thought, she added, "I want you to accept his request."

"May I ask why?"

"While Malette's family believe House Escariot is after my life, they will not hire anyone else. That way, it will buy us some time to get the Duke on trial for his crimes and destroy his reputation."

He smirked. "Very clever, Master."

"Have someone watch the family's movements and who they associate with. I need to know what they are plotting."

"I have assigned a shadow to their household. Please be at ease."

She got up and walked to him. Placing her hand on his wide chest, she felt his heart racing under her palm. "Remember to stop peeping at ladies when they are changing. Such hobbies are beneath you, Clayton."

The tips of his ears reddened, and he stepped out of her reach. "I will keep that in mind."

"One more thing. I believe Julio is hiding in the catacombs under the palace. Speak with Ambrose. She will guide you."

"Will do, Your Majesty."

"Good day to you, Lord Armel."

He got the hint and produced a heart-stopping smile. "Goodbye, my master."

She watched as he left through the balcony. Her heart fluttered in her chest. Had they met under different circumstances, she might have asked him out on a date. Clayton was too good-looking for an unwed woman to pass up.

As Queen, she could not allow fleeting feelings such as love to sprout. Love and trust were weaknesses that brought down the most powerful monarchs throughout history. She could not afford to become one of them. Not when her ultimate goal was to survive and live a carefree life.

Once Emilia made sure no one else was eager to discuss matters of the state with her, she had the maids pour her a bath.

She climbed into the rose-scented water that soothed the aches all over her tired body. Although she had only recently become a monarch, she already needed a holiday. Living her life as an unwanted princess had its perks. No one disturbed her much, nor had any expectations of her aside from fulfilling her filial duty and getting married to some old lord somewhere.

Emilia closed her eyes and enjoyed the quiet. Her thoughts slowed until she succumbed to sleep.

"Your Majesty! Are you alright?" Ambrose's shrieks startled Emilia.

Emilia's eyes burst open. She was still in the bath. The water had long since gotten cold.

She rubbed her eyes. "Did I fall asleep?"

"Please get out of the cold water. I will bring you clothes and some hot soup to warm you up. I should call on Mister Benjamin to—"

"Calm down. I am perfectly fine. I must have dozed off."

Ambrose helped Emilia out of the bath and hurriedly wrapped a cotton towel around Emilia's body.

"Do not take a bath on your own, Your Majesty. What would I do if something were to happen to you?"

"I won't do it again. Will that make you happy?"

Ambrose bobbed her head, but her expression remained stern, like that of a mother who found her child partaking in dangerous deeds.

Ushered out of the bathroom, Emilia was forced under the bedcovers while Ambrose ran around the room with purpose.

Once Ambrose organised everything, she assisted Emilia in putting her clothes on and arranging her raven hair into a braid. Right after, Ambrose left and came back with a steaming bowl of mushroom soup, rye bread, and a pot of black tea on a large silver tray.

Beaming, Ambrose offered the soup to Emilia. "Please eat, Your Majesty. You need to warm up your body."

Emilia did not dare to argue. When Ambrose was in her motherly mode, nothing she could say would get her maid to quit. It was faster to allow the girl to attend to her until Ambrose was satisfied.

Taking her time, Emilia polished off a bowl of tasty soup and moved on to drinking her tea. The chill from the cold bath was gone, just like that.

"Did you speak to Lord Armel?"

Her maid tucked a stray wisp of her brown hair behind her ear. "I have, Your Majesty. I told him everything I observed last night in the west wing."

"Did you find the secret passage?"

"There is a lever hidden behind a painting of King Gilebert riding a black steed."

Emilia felt her lips curving upwards. "Did he say what he is planning to do next?"

"Lord Armel will explore the passageways with Lady Isobelle and return with a detailed map. He does not plan to approach Julio Grande unless he believes he can capture him with ease."

"Good thing he took backup with him. I believe we may need a group of people to inspect the catacombs. Who knows what traps Julio and the late king have laid out? I hope the Armel siblings will come back alive."

"Do you hold affection for him, Your Majesty?"

Emilia nearly choked on her tea. "I think he is useful. Why?"

"He seems quite fond of you."

"Lord Armel only sees me as his master. His curse prevents him from disobeying me, forcing him to act that way."

Ambrose tilted her head to one side. "He does not appear as if

150

he is forced to do anything. Lord Armel seems to smile whenever I mention you, Your Majesty."

Emilia let out a giggle as she dismissed Ambrose's observation. Her maid had read too many romance novels in private. Ambrose had recently turned twenty and was at the age where she should look for a suitable man to fall in love with. One day, Emilia would help her maid settle down if Ambrose so desired.

"Clayton and I are comrades, nothing more. I will help him break his curse in return for his loyalty. Do not think too deeply about this matter."

"I must have been mistaken."

Emilia drank the rest of her tea in silence as she contemplated the news of the discovered secret passage. "Inform Lionhart, Sir Laurence, Dame Cali, Lady Riga, and Prince Thessian to come fully armed to the west wing after dinner. There is a rat we must corner."

20

A LADY'S FEELINGS

THESSIAN

After an exhausting day, Thessian returned to the palace. He took a long bath to wash away the stench of smoke and layers of dirt off his body.

A servant brought him a hearty meal to fill his stomach.

He never shied away from manual labour, but it had been a while. A night of hard work had caused his muscles to burn, especially his thigh. He contemplated retrieving a magical healing potion from his storage at camp. The three vials he had cost an arm and a leg to procure from the Mage Assembly, but he needed to get back to his full strength.

In the back of his mind, he wondered how Laurence was holding up. His friend was demoted and pushed out of the elite unit. As a leader, Thessian had to make tough decisions. But, as Laurence's childhood friend, he felt bitter about the ordeal. He could only hope

Emilia would not find out about the origins of the fire.

Then again, if she can see the future, perhaps she knew the truth long before it happened.

Thessian raked his fingers through his messy, blond hair. *Is there any need to keep it a secret from her?*

He secured his belt around his waist and sheathed his weapons in their respective places—two daggers in his boots and a sword at his hip. Blowing out a breath, he left his room.

Down the hall, he came across Lady Riga, who was heading towards him.

"Good afternoon, Lady Riga."

She curtsied. "Greetings, Your Grace. I heard there was a great fire in the city. Do you know anything about the situation?"

Thessian could not help smiling. Riga got down to business rather quickly for someone her age. That trait made her as straightforward as Lord Fournier.

"There is no need to worry. We have taken care of the fire."

She placed her hand over her heart. "It is reassuring to hear you say that."

He looked around. "Are you going somewhere?"

"I plan to take a stroll in the inner garden. My body has gotten stiff from staying in my room."

"Would you like for me to accompany you?"

She perked up at his suggestion. "That would be quite an honour!"

He worked hard to keep pace with her short stride. She was a few inches shorter than Emilia, making it hard for him not to run ahead of her every time he got distracted by a stray thought.

They entered the garden.

The sun beat down on them from high above and the chill was subsiding. He could not wait for the snow to melt.

Lady Riga came to a stop. "Do you hear that, Your Grace?"

Thessian strained his ears and picked up on the sound of someone crying. "Sounds like it is none of our business."

"But what if they are hurt or in trouble?"

He sighed. "Lead the way."

Riga ran ahead, finally allowing him to resume his normal pace.

Near the fountain at the back of the garden, they found Cali hunched over on a bench.

Thessian stopped in front of his subordinate. "What is the matter, Cali?"

She froze and wiped at her tear-streaked face. "Nothing, Your Highness. I got some dirt in my eye..."

Lady Riga pouted. "There must be a boulder in your eye for you to cry so hard."

Cali sniffled and stood to attention. Her eyes were red and puffy from what seemed to be a long bout of crying.

Thessian was in two minds about prying. He tested the waters. "Would you like to tell us what has upset you?"

"Do not worry, Your Highness. This will not affect my work."

"Very good," he mumbled.

"Mama said that if a lady refuses to speak, it must be related to men. Who is the uneducated swine with poor judgement to make you this miserable?"

Thessian's mouth fell open at the language Lady Riga used.

Cali, too, seemed utterly astounded.

Lady Riga blushed. "Your Grace, please give us ladies some space."

Sensing his chance to escape, he replied, "I will be on my way."

He strode away, all the while trying to figure out what could be wrong with Cali.

Is she unhappy with her new position?

It was a lot of work, and she needed to stay close to him.

Lady Riga mentioned a problem with a man.

Does she dislike the idea of being close to me?

Until now, Dame Cali spent most of her time around Laurence and the other knights. She acted a tad intimidated when Thessian was around. That had to be the cause of her breakdown.

Satisfied with his conclusion, the prince made a mental note to be more approachable the next time they met.

21
THE DEAL

EMILIA

The day dragged on, yet Emilia's paperwork pile showed no improvement. She wondered if she was the only one in the kingdom doing all the work. The nobles who were meant to support her were busy organising private parties and teatime with friends.

Resting her chin on her palm, she flicked through the pages of a proposal for a road investment through Baron Niel's territory. It would increase the speed of goods being delivered to Newburn, but the construction cost was too steep.

Based on Lionhart's information, Baron Niel was an opportunist. He supported Emilia in her plans to overthrow King Gilebert without putting in much effort. A two-faced man like him would use the gold for bolstering his private army while using the cheapest possible materials to complete the road.

She pushed the proposal aside. Deciding without additional information could pose more problems down the line.

The guard, Antonio, announced that Dame Cali wished for an audience.

Emilia rejoiced at the opportunity to push her work aside. "Let her in."

Cali entered the office with her eyes completely swollen. "Your Majesty, I apologise for the intrusion. I wish to inform you I can no longer fulfil my role as Guard Captain."

"Perfect timing." Emilia sat back in her seat and smiled. "I have someone lined up for the position. In the interim, I still require you to fill in the role until that person arrives."

"Very well. That is all I came to say."

"Is Prince Thessian going to assign someone else to be by my side?"

"I am not aware of that, Your Majesty."

Emilia tapped her index finger on her desk. Thessian had yet to fully put his trust in her abilities. He was bound to keep watch over her every move.

Unless he is observing me in secret…

No. Thessian believed she could see the future. Doing something like that would seem pointless to him.

"May I ask where you are being stationed, Dame Cali?"

"I am to take over Sir Laurence's post as His Highness' second-in-command."

Emilia kept a straight face. In the novel, Thessian and Laurence often had playful arguments, but never any serious fallouts.

Is Laurence being reassigned, or did he do something terribly wrong?
"Where will Sir Laurence go?"

"I cannot divulge such details without His Highness' permission." Cali bowed her head and backed out of the room.

Well, Cali clammed up rather quickly.

Based on Cali's depressed appearance and the sudden change in command, Emilia smelled a tremendous secret. She felt her lips stretching into a grin. Since Cali would not share any information, that left Laurence and Thessian.

Getting up from her desk, she calculated where they could be.

Thessian would be resting after helping with the fire, and Laurence was either at camp or nearby. She went with the surer option and hurried to Thessian's room in the palace.

The paperwork can wait.

Her guess paid off.

She knocked three times before hearing footsteps, and His Highness opened the door.

Dressed in a pair of trousers and a tight linen shirt, he seemed like any normal hot guy who was taking a day off work. As she craned her neck to look at his gorgeous face, all she could think about was that his fandom's illustrations did not do him justice. Nonetheless, the author did a fine job creating a perfect specimen. Sometimes, it was a struggle for Emilia to not turn into a screaming fangirl around him.

"I wish to speak with you in private, Your Highness."

He made a sweeping motion as he opened the door wider. "Please, come inside."

She followed his words and heard the door closing behind her.

Putting on her best poker face, she faced him. "I *saw* what happened..."

Thessian's eyes widened a fraction. He blew out a sigh as he rubbed the back of his neck. "I see there is no way to keep this from you."

"I cannot believe Laurence did that," she added in a grim voice while keeping her eyes on his reactions. The odds of Laurence making a mistake were higher than being reassigned out of the blue. Thessian would not force Laurence to step down from his position otherwise.

"I knew you would find out eventually," he admitted. "I will take responsibility for what happened to your city. Rest assured, Laurence and the other squad leaders were punished for this mistake too."

City? Did Thessian's men cause the fire?

Her legs nearly gave out. She stumbled upon a huge bombshell.

"How do you plan to atone for this? I may be a mere regent, but

157

I am also a daughter of this nation. My people suffered, some even died because of yesterday's calamity!"

Thessian winced. He lowered his head, an action that did not help him look any smaller. "I could compensate you for the damage caused."

Emilia did not wish to tarnish their relationship, but forgiving him easily would make her seem weak. "First, tell me about their punishment."

Their eyes met.

"I have stripped them of their rank. Laurence and Ian are due to leave Newburn in the coming weeks."

Sir Laurence is truly leaving Thessian's side? The plot of the novel had completely derailed from the original.

"Are they returning to Darkgate?" she asked.

"No. They received an assignment to track a member of the beastmen."

She gasped. "There are more of them?"

"I believe there may be some remnants within Dante's territory."

Emilia cared little for the beastmen. They were a reclusive group that was destroyed by the avarice of neighbouring kingdoms and largely forgotten by history. Whether Laurence found them or not was unimportant.

"Instead of compensation, I want Your Highness to be honest with me from now on. For the foreseeable future, we are partners, and partnerships are built on trust."

"Does that mean you will put *your* trust in me also?"

"Of course."

"Shall we resume our previous conversation? I have told you about myself. You know all of my weak points. And yet, I know next to nothing about you, Emilia. Are you willing to tell me about yourself this time?"

She looked away. "There is nothing to tell. My life has been quite boring, I assure you."

He crossed his arms. "Somehow, I do not believe that."

Emilia dug her own grave. She wanted him to put his faith in her while she could not muster the courage to return the favour.

Swallowing the knot in her throat, she spoke low. "What would you like to know?"

"Did you love your family?"

"Nothing about them or how they treated me warranted such a grand emotion."

"What about your friends?"

"What about them?"

"How did you meet them?"

.A sigh of frustration escaped her, and she looked around his room. There was nowhere to hide.

"I took in Ambrose from an orphanage and met Lionhart by doing business with his guild. My visions were quite useful to him."

His eyes wrinkled at the corners when he smiled. "I am pleased to know you think of them as your friends and not your subjects."

A deep frown set on her brow. "You are making very little sense."

"You are equally mysterious to me."

A blush crept up to her cheeks. "Are you satisfied with my answers? I have work to return to."

When she inched towards the door, he blocked her escape.

"How about a fair trade? I will ask you one personal question a day, and you can ask anything you want in return."

"I—" she swallowed nervously, "—will do my best to oblige."

22

PREPARATIONS

EMILIA

Right before dinner, Clayton and Isobelle returned from their scouting mission and reported to Emilia's office.

Emilia studied the state of their clothes. Dust coated every inch of their bodies. Clayton even had a cobweb or two tangled in his hair.

She stifled a giggle. The siblings had worked hard. She couldn't possibly make them feel embarrassed on purpose.

After clearing her throat, Emilia said, "Tell me what you have found."

Clayton rummaged in his leather satchel and pulled out a parchment with a carefully sketched map, which he spread out on her desk.

"This is what we uncovered once we descended into the secret passage, Your Majesty." He pointed to the twisting passages that looked like spaghetti. "There are a lot of paths that lead to a sizeable central chamber. We could not enter. The doors had some kind of enchantment placed on them. We believe only those of the royal bloodline can pass."

Emilia tilted her head to one side. "Then how would Julio get in?"

"He may have King Gilebert's blood or hair."

A feasible answer.

For a king who pretended to hate magic on the surface, Gilebert seemed eager to spend a fortune on magical enchantments. No wonder the kingdom had a laughable amount of gold left.

"Did you find any traps down there?"

"No, Your Majesty. We traversed the passages that are used the most. Based on the footprints left behind, we believe someone is helping Julio Grande."

"Hmm." Emilia kept her attention on the map, allowing herself a minute to memorize it.

A stern knock on the door alerted her to Sir Rowell's entrance. "Your Majesty, dinner is served. Prince Thessian and Lady Riga are waiting for you in the dining room."

"Prepare two more plates. Viscount Armel and his sister will join us."

"Yes, Your Majesty."

Emilia quickly added, "Sir Rowell, do you know of any palace staff who often go missing in the west wing?"

The old butler drew his thick, grey brows together. "The servants saw Roderick slacking off there, Your Majesty. May I ask why you are looking into this? I have already assigned a punishment for him."

"Someone is helping a criminal within these walls. I hope you understand that this information must not leave this room."

"What would you have me do?" the head butler asked readily.

With each passing day, Emilia grew fonder of Sir Rowell. He was eager to help and never asked for anything in return—a perfect servant.

"Detain this Roderick without anyone's notice."

Lady Isobelle stepped forward. "Your Majesty, it is rather late. Could you permit us to stay the night at the palace?"

Even covered in dirt and dust, Isobelle looked like a beautiful rogue. Emilia could not help stealing glances at the lady's refined face and perfectly symmetric bone structure. As a noble, Lady Isobelle probably had suitors lining up to high heaven.

"Sir Rowell," Emilia began, "have the servants prepare rooms for my guests."

The head butler nodded and slipped out of the room.

Emilia smiled at Isobelle. "Have a meal with me and then get some rest. You two have worked hard today."

"It is our duty to serve you," Isobelle replied. "Your Majesty, may I make a request?"

"I'm listening."

"Could I decline your invitation? I would prefer to not sully Your Majesty's image by attending a dinner with other nobles in such a dishevelled state."

Emilia pinched the bridge of her nose. How could she forget that a noble's image was the most important thing to them? She was forcing a viscount and a noblewoman to attend a dinner with foreign royalty.

"I will have the servants bring the food to your rooms," Emilia offered.

Isobelle perked up. "Thank you for your benevolence!"

Clayton's silence drew Emilia's attention. "You seem just as pleased to avoid dinner with me, Lord Armel."

His cheeks reddened. "There is no such thing, Your Majesty."

"I jest."

Isobelle covered her growing smile with her hand. "Brother must be disappointed. He could not stop talking about our master the entire time we were underground."

Clayton glared at his sister. "Please disregard my sister's insolent words. Isobelle has been indoors for a long time and must have forgotten what should not be said in polite company."

Isobelle pouted. "I did not lie!"

Seeing two siblings who got along brought a smile to Emilia's face. If only her deceased brothers were like Isobelle or Clayton.

Would my life be any different? Would the hurt in my heart be less?

Emilia folded the map Clayton gave her and stashed it in the inner pocket of her dress as she rose to her full height. "I best not keep my guests waiting for much longer. Have a good rest, Lord Armel, Lady Isobelle."

The siblings said their goodbyes and exited her office.

Emilia looked back at her desk.

Will a day come when I no longer feel trapped in here?

Facing Thessian and Lady Riga at the long dinner table, Emilia picked at the peas on her plate. She contemplated how she was going to bring up Julio Grande to Thessian without him getting angry.

Thessian broke the silence first, after he wiped his spotless mouth with a napkin. "May I ask why it is you want to gather everyone in the west wing?"

Emilia set her cutlery down and reached for her glass of wine. She took a small sip to wet her suddenly parched throat. "There is a situation we must deal with."

He remained quiet, waiting for her to continue.

"I did not wish to ruin your appetite with this matter. It involves Julio Grande."

Thessian's body visibly tensed. "Has he arrived at the palace?"

"Although Lord Armel discreetly delivered him here, Mister Grande broke away from the guards and disappeared in the west wing. Not long ago, the Armel siblings returned after exploring a secret passageway. So, I would like for everyone to take part in the search."

Emilia's words were only partially a lie. As long as the prince got his hands on Julio, she doubted he cared for the fine details. Concurrently, she could not throw Clayton under the carriage and blame the circumstances entirely on him.

Thessian violently cut into his steak. "Are you certain he is still there?"

Emilia imagined Thessian cutting her throat with that knife instead of the meat. "T-there is a large central chamber under the palace that my father built. I believe Mister Grande has been hiding there to avoid being seen."

He stopped what he was doing. Although they had grown closer, he had plenty of doubts in his eyes to burn a village. "I hope this issue will be resolved by tonight."

As do I! She wanted to yell.

The fact that the original novel never mentioned Julio or his connection to King Gilebert annoyed her to no end.

How could the author omit something so important?

Emilia could have prepared in advance and gained Thessian's trust much faster. As things stood, Thessian's distrust in her abilities was returning. She could not afford for anything to go wrong during their trip into the catacombs.

Lady Riga glanced from Thessian to Emilia. "Your Grace, may I ask what it is you are talking about?"

"It is a personal matter of mine," Thessian replied. "There is someone we must apprehend, and I would appreciate your help."

"Of course, Your Grace," the young girl said.

Taking another sip of the sweet wine, Emilia assessed Riga over the rim of her goblet. For a child, Riga acted maturely. Too bad her loyalties lay with the prince. Emilia would never say no to a fire mage being on her side.

Luckily, Thessian wanted to secure a magic tutor for Riga. Under Clayton's wing, Riga would prosper as a mage, and he could monitor the child.

Lord Fournier had a strong military presence up north. If Riga shifted her support to Emilia, the Fourniers might be open to supporting her too.

Emilia softened her expression. "Lady Riga, I believe I have found a magic tutor for you."

Riga's face lit up. "You have?"

"He is quite skilled, and I am positive you two will get along."

Thessian scowled. "I am not in full agreement with your decision."

"Do you believe he is unqualified, Your Highness?"

"You know exactly why he may be a problematic choice."

Emilia smirked. "Oh? And why is that?"

Thessian was about to say something and stopped when he noticed Riga's intent stare. "Nothing."

Emilia clasped her hands. "Splendid! I will introduce the young lady to him."

Thessian's disapproving glare burned into Emilia's face, and she chose to ignore it.

After the meal, Emilia got ready in her room.

She changed into new clothes that were much more comfortable and easier to move in than a heavy dress.

Months ago, she sent a request to a tailor affiliated with the Lionhart Guild to create a new outfit for her. The beautiful royal blue brocade of her military-style coat shimmered with silver and gold threads. She fixed her gaze on the edelweiss flowers that were embroidered with precision, symbolizing the courage she needed to continue on her path. The coat matched well with her form-fitting black trousers.

She tied her hair into a long ponytail and selected two daggers, which she hid in her boots. As she sheathed her shortsword around her waist, she smirked at her reflection in the mirror.

"You seem to be in a good mood, Your Majesty," Ambrose pointed out.

"Is it obvious?"

"Somewhat."

Emilia took hold of her maid's hands. "You know me best. Take care of things in the palace while we are underground."

Ambrose's fingers tightened around Emilia's. "I would prefer to accompany you."

"There is no need to worry. We will return shortly. I am certain of it."

"How can you be so sure?"

The most skilled people in the kingdom would accompany Emilia. There was no way Julio could beat them unless he was secretly a mage.

"Call it a gut feeling."

"Then, I will wait for Your Majesty's safe return."

Emilia's heart warmed. Ambrose's unshakeable loyalty was more precious than any jewel or sheet of priceless fabric. She couldn't help pulling Ambrose into a tight hug.

"I will come back." With that, Emilia drew back and headed to the west wing.

Thessian and the others came into Emilia's view, and she broke into a smile. Being a character in a novel was not all bad. She got to meet the characters she once held dear. Seeing them living and breathing made her heart race.

"Your Majesty," Clayton called behind her.

Emilia peered over her shoulder. He had changed his clothes and must have had a bath, since his hair was damp and slicked back.

"What are you doing here, Lord Armel?"

He stopped a courteous distance away. Even then, she had to crane her neck to look at his face. "I cannot let my master go in there without protection."

She pointed to the group of people up ahead. "I am not going in alone."

"If you would allow it, I wish to accompany you."

"Are you not tired?"

"I am fine."

Emilia could not turn him down when he looked like a dejected puppy. Yet, as a leader, she did not want him to keep pushing his limits to prove he was of use to her.

Is the curse forcing him to be so desperate?

Regardless of her decision, she knew he would follow her into the catacombs.

"Do as you like."

Clayton broke into a smile. "Thank you."

If only I could bottle that smile and those looks, it would make a fortune among the single ladies. Surely, Clayton had a lot of admirers hiding away somewhere or a fiancée.

Shaking off strange thoughts, Emilia joined the rest of the group with Clayton in tow.

She smiled brightly at the faces that were filled with interest. "I have gathered you here to help in the capture of a criminal who has hidden in the catacombs."

After pulling out the map Clayton and Isobelle had drawn, she showed it to the others.

"As you can see, three main passageways lead to a single central chamber. I believe the man in question is hiding there."

"Would that be Julio Grande, Your Majesty?" Dame Cali inquired.

Emilia nodded. "Since you are here, Lord Armel, fill them in on the details."

Clayton stepped forward. "My sister and I traversed these passageways and found a door that leads to the central chamber, which is sealed with magic. We believe that only those of royal blood may break the seal. There are no visible traps and some rodents. We spotted nothing else out of the ordinary."

Thessian frowned. He looked just as intimidating in his dark leather armour as he did on the first night of their meeting. "There is no way Julio Grande is of Dante's royal blood."

"No, he is not," Emilia confirmed. "I suspect he possesses a vial with my father's blood or something in the same vein. Therefore, I am going down the main path towards the seal. The rest of you will split up and guard the other paths in case Julio emerges. Of course, there is no guarantee that there isn't another passage we have overlooked."

"I shall go with you," Thessian said.

"Very well. Lord Armel and His Highness will come with me."

Emilia spotted Riga. *It would be a good idea for Lionhart to evaluate her abilities.* "Lionhart can accompany Lady Riga, and Sir Laurence will take Dame Cali."

Laurence scratched the back of his neck. "I would prefer to be paired with Lady Riga."

That's unexpected. Weren't Laurence and Cali from the same unit? Judging by how awkward he's behaving, and the physical distance between them, they must have fought.

Emilia pressed her lips into a tight line. Laurence had burned down a part of her city and dared to make demands?

Thessian spoke before Emilia could add anything. "Escort Lady Riga, Laurence. Cali, you are with the spymaster."

They accepted His Highness' command without complaint.

Emilia glanced at Lionhart and wordlessly told him to be careful. Then she clasped her hands together and announced, "Shall we get going?"

23
COMRADERY

LAURENCE

Laurence clutched the lantern's handle, lighting the path ahead of him and the young lady. They had split off from the others a short while ago, giving him room to breathe. Being around Calithea was too awkward. He should not have taken his anger out on her. She didn't deserve it.

He let out a heavy sigh.

"Sir Laurence, is something bothering you?" Riga was barely past his elbow in height. When dressed in her equestrian attire, her body seemed so slim he feared she would break in half from a gust of wind. Good thing they were underground.

"I am fine," he said with a fake smile.

Laurence kept his attention on the winding tunnels ahead. Hardly anyone used the path they took. There were some footprints in the dirt, which he assumed belonged to the scouting party before them.

Halfway down the path, the granite walls changed to an unknown greenish stone that had strange hieroglyphs carved into it. The stale air made him feel as though they were deep within a forgotten tomb.

"Do you hate Dame Cali?"

Riga's question had him pause. He finally looked at the child, seeing a pair of eyes filled with curiosity rather than judgement.

"I do not hate her. She is my comrade."

"Dame Cali believes you do."

Laurence's jaw ached from how hard he clenched it. "Lady Riga, what are you implying?"

She smiled, lighting up her round, childlike face. "I wish for us all to get along."

"We get along just fine."

He strode ahead. To his surprise, she said nothing else.

Laurence blocked out the thoughts about Cali as much as he could and focused on the directions given by Her Majesty. Emilia differed from any royalty he had met. He could not decide whether she was a reckless genius or had the God of Luck on her side. With her ability to *See*, His Highness could ascend the throne of Hellion in no time.

That is, if Emilia is being truthful. If her ability was Deception instead of Sight, Prince Thessian could be in danger.

And if I leave...

Lady Riga grabbed his sleeve and tugged on it. "Sir Laurence, please shorten your stride! I cannot keep up!"

"Ah, my apologies."

She peered past him, and her eyes widened. "What's that?"

Upon turning around, Laurence discovered they came to a drawn drawbridge. Judging by its appearance, it seems to have been built within the last ten years.

He walked up to the end of their path and dangled his lantern over the seemingly bottomless pit.

Riga scooted closer to him. "How deep do you think it goes?"

Instinctively, he pushed her away from the edge. "It is too

dangerous for you, my lady. Please stand back from the edge."

She bobbed her head, making her messy blonde curls dance around her shoulders.

Did Count Fournier forget to assign a maid to accompany the poor girl?

Laurence picked up a palm-sized stone and tossed it into the pit. He counted several seconds before it clanged against the rocks below.

"It would be best to avoid falling," he commented.

"You are probably right." Lady Riga produced a ball of fire as large as her head above her palm.

"What are you—"

Before he could finish, she fired the ball into the darkness. As it descended, he could see the sharp edges and spikes of the protruding rock formations of the cliff they found themselves on.

At the very bottom, as the fire extinguished itself, he glimpsed human remains that were discarded in the pit without a care.

He grimaced.

"Did you see something, Sir Laurence?"

Best not to tell her. "Nothing of note. I think we should get away from the edge. There is nothing here."

She pointed at the drawbridge. "Shouldn't we try to lower that?"

"If we do, it may alert our target."

"Then, do we wait for Mister Grande, in case he attempts to escape this way?"

For a child, Lady Riga had a good head on her shoulders. No wonder Lord Fournier had no qualms about sending her off at the age of twelve.

"Yes, my lady. Let us find a place to rest where we won't be seen from the other side of the bridge."

24

THE HEART OF DANTE

EMILIA

Emilia had memorized the layout of the catacombs and their passages, yet being deep underground was a completely different story. She kept her eyes trained on the path illuminated by Thessian's lantern.

The sight of cobwebs and the tiny skeletons of rodents twisted her stomach into knots. She hoped that after escaping the tower, she could avoid such dreary sights. Although she was merely a character in a book someone wrote, years of torment and abuse by her supposed family were hard to erase.

Clayton matched her pace and gently took hold of her fingertips. In a low voice, he said, "Your hand is shaking, Your Majesty."

She jerked her hand away. "You must be imagining things."

The grey in his irises appeared almost black in the dim light.

Clayton smiled weakly. "I must have been mistaken."

Emilia peeked at her clenched fist. Even after he had removed his hand, the coolness of his touch remained on her skin. She could not appear weak in front of these men. Even though Clayton had sworn loyalty, she couldn't shake the feeling that he would turn against her once his curse was lifted. Thessian, too, would stop taking her seriously if she showed how uncomfortable she was in the dark and cramped spaces.

Should I have escaped the main story by running away with Ambrose and her sister?

Emilia had thought long and hard about every eventuality. The best thing for the story was for Thessian or his older brother, Cain, to ascend to the throne of the Hellion Empire. Prince Kyros would plunge the continent into endless bloodshed and kill all of the mages on the path of his conquest. As a war-hungry tyrant, it made sense for Kyros to eliminate those with the power to oppose him. To prevent any potential uprisings, even children born into mage families would be quickly disposed of. No place on the continent would be safe. Helping Thessian was the only path with a chance of a bright future.

"I think we are almost there," Thessian announced.

Emilia spied an outline of curved stone doors the size of the castle's main gates.

When they got closer, she could make out more details. The greenish stone was covered in rows upon rows of ancient text, resembling those on Clayton's back.

"I can sense a strong magic barrier here, Your Majesty." Clayton hovered his hand an inch away from the door. "Be careful not to touch it carelessly."

From the corner of her eye, she saw Thessian withdrawing his hand.

Clayton must have directed his warning at the prince.

"How do we open it? Do I cut myself and bleed on it?" she asked.

Clayton offered his hand. "May I hold your hand, Your Majesty?"

Thessian crossed his arms. "Hurry and open this door, mage.

We cannot let that lunatic get away."

For a second, Emilia thought she saw anger fleeting across Clayton's face.

She placed her hand in Clayton's palm, and he gently smiled at her.

Turning her hand, palm up, he traced his index finger over the fingertip of her middle finger. As he did that, a cool sensation spread across her palm.

He moved his hand away, and a drop of her blood crystallized on her fingertip.

"Wow. It did not hurt at all," she murmured.

Clayton picked up the bead of her blood and touched it against the door.

Suddenly, the air grew thick, and she heard a loud mechanism clanking inside the wall.

There is no way Julio won't hear us coming.

The enormous doors sluggishly pulled apart.

One look at the thickness of the doors told her it would have been impossible to get in without modern-day drilling machinery or a catapult. Whoever designed this place didn't want anyone coming in without a royal invitation.

Thessian grinned with malice and unsheathed his sword. "Finally!"

"Stay behind us, Your Majesty," Clayton said, holding an ice dagger. "We do not know what kind of welcome awaits us."

Emilia followed suit by drawing two of her daggers. "I know you are eager to catch Julio, Your Highness, but please be careful."

Thessian peered over his shoulder at her. His expression softened. "Yes, I should not allow my emotions to get the best of me here."

Emilia returned his smile.

The prince cautiously strode ahead, leading the way with the lantern raised high.

Slowly, they progressed farther inside. Each of their steps echoed in the nervous silence.

As she continued walking, the darkness gave way to flickering torches lining the stone walls. The hieroglyphs etched onto the lengthy walls gave off an ominous vibe, as if telling them to turn back.

The long passageway led to a huge circular chamber, which was even grander than the throne room. Thick black pillars supported a ceiling so high that the light from the torches could not reach it.

How could such a grand place fit under the palace?

Were we going down the entire time without realising it?

There was no way King Gilebert built this place in five years without anyone noticing. From a quick examination, the materials used for construction were ancient and scarce on the continent. The twenty pillars appeared to be made of rare black quartz. The price tag for such a mineral would have bankrupted Dante ten times over.

King Gilebert always focused on outward appearances. He would not spend a fortune on a chamber that no one would ever see. Emilia's tower was a great example of that. From the outside, it appeared to be a white tower with a gold-tipped roof, but the inside was filled with old furniture and bats.

Thessian abruptly came to a halt.

Emilia sensed the tension in his body rising as he tightened the grip on his sword and looked ahead.

She stuck her head around the two tall, broad-shouldered men.

The middle of the chamber housed a cage large enough to fit an overgrown elephant. Her gaze immediately fell upon the source of her companion's distress.

A small boy lay inside the cage without a single thread of material to cover or warm him. Thick metal shackles held his limbs firmly, the weight of which was too much for his thin body.

"Who would do such a thing?" she asked no one in particular.

Thessian's voice trembled with outrage. "This is Grande's work!"

Emilia studied his face. A vein had popped out on the prince's forehead as he audibly ground his teeth.

"Are you speaking from experience, Your Highness?"

"When I caught him in the past, I was the one who freed the

children he tortured. Few survived, and even fewer remained sane."

Clayton did not show the same empathy that overwhelmed her or Thessian. In Emilia's eyes, the assassin seemed more focused on his dagger, as if expecting an attack at any moment.

A wry smile stretched her lips. Clayton was a character she had never read about in the story. Had she not become Queen, he would be free of his curse.

Does he not resent me?

"I will search for the culprit," Thessian informed her.

Before he could split off from the group, she put away her daggers and grasped the prince by the hand. "What should we do with the boy?"

"He is a victim in all of this, but he must be a mage if they have restrained him to such a degree. Be cautious."

She let go, and Thessian left through another arched doorway.

Emilia quietly approached the boy with Clayton checking for traps that would protect the cage from intruders.

After a while, she was close enough to make out the frail boy clearly.

How could a human being treat a child with such cruelty?

She now completely understood why Thessian was hell-bent on capturing Julio and ending his abhorrent research.

"Child, can you hear me?" she crooned. "Are you hurt?"

The boy did not respond.

She could not see his face. His wavy auburn hair concealed it from view.

The boy's chest rose and fell with steady breaths.

He was alive.

"Lord Armel, can you break the lock on this cage?"

"Your Majesty, are you certain you wish to open it without proper protection? I could return here with Isobelle and deal with the boy later."

"We cannot leave him like this! He has suffered enough."

"The prince said that many children lost their minds after Grande's experimentation. This may be a similar case."

"I will take responsibility. Open the cage."

From the inner pocket of his coat, Clayton retrieved a leather satchel that contained a set of lock-picking tools similar to the one she often carried. It did not take long for him to produce a satisfying click from the heavy lock.

"Step back, Your Majesty. I will open the door."

Emilia moved three steps away from the cage. To seem harmless to the child, she kept her hands at her sides.

Clayton blew out a breath and pushed the metal door open with an ear-splitting squeal of the hinges.

Once the cage opened, he stepped inside and checked the restraints on the boy's arms.

Upon unlocking the child's wrists, Clayton's eyes widened in shock. "Your Majesty, run!"

As his words registered in her mind, and Clayton propelled himself out of the cage, she stumbled backwards. She could not tear her eyes away from the boy, who was quickly morphing into a huge monstrosity faster than her nervous breaths could reach her lungs.

Clayton grasped her by the shoulders and pulled her away.

The shackles, that once kept the boy tethered, melted away. The metal bars of the cage bent and buckled under the weight of the monster, none other than a black-scaled dragon she had read about in fables.

The dragon let out a loud screech in warning.

Emilia's heart thudded in her chest. Even then, Clayton had his arms wrapped tightly around her waist and kept moving her away from the beast.

"Your Majesty, you must get out of here!" Clayton spoke into her ear when they reached one of the sturdy pillars.

She squeaked in disbelief. "Is that what I think it is?"

"I will distract it while you make your escape."

Emilia regained her composure once she noticed how Clayton's voice trembled. "We cannot allow that thing to stay here."

"We cannot fight against it!" he informed her. "My remaining mana will not be enough."

One look at the beast told her it was intelligent. It did not charge them blindly, nor was it going on a rampage after breaking out of its confinement. Its golden eyes followed their every move as they crouched behind the pillar, contemplating their next move.

How did Julio and King Gilebert keep such a dangerous creature in check?

She could not see any control crystals that could explain its docile behaviour until their arrival.

Emilia swallowed her nerves. "I'll try speaking to it."

Clayton squeezed her hand. "It is too dangerous. I cannot allow my master to be put in such danger."

"Don't worry. If I die, you will be free from your curse. You can get out of here and never look back."

He yanked her back and grasped her by the shoulders. "Do you think so little of my loyalty to you?"

Honestly, she did not know what to make of Clayton's servitude. Had she been in his shoes, she would no doubt constantly wish for freedom. Being cursed from a young age to serve some master was bound to make bad blood build up over the years.

She pushed him away. "Remember your place, Lord Armel."

An undecipherable emotion fleeted across his face. He lowered his head and fisted his hands at his sides.

"Forgive my rudeness, Your Majesty. No matter what may happen, I will be your shield."

25
DEAD END

THESSIAN

Having split off from Emilia and the assassin, Thessian roamed the winding corridors. He checked every room along the way in case Julio was there.

The rooms had traces of occupancy in recent months. Among the scarce furniture suitable for young children, he found over a dozen discarded nightgowns. Julio had to be running his experiments in Dante since his escape from the Empire.

One room remained at the end of the long corridor. With each step, his heart beat faster, and his jaw clenched tighter. He could hear the hurried shuffling of papers and someone's cussing in the Empire's tongue.

He sucked in a deep breath and put all of his weight into kicking the flimsy door open.

The wooden obstacle flew off the hinges and fell with a thud.

Standing next to a desk that was overflowing with parchments and splattered ink was the man Thessian had been searching for.

Julio had lost some weight since their last encounter. His soulless eyes had sunk deeper into his head. A full head of once blond hair had long since lost its shine and became spotted with clumps of grey.

"Y-you c-cannot be here..." Julio stammered over his words. His eyes darted from Thessian, who blocked the only way out, to his messy desk.

"Why ever not?" Thessian snarled. "Thought you escaped punishment for all the atrocities you have committed?"

Julio raised his hands in defence. "I-I only did what I was told."

Thessian let out a bitter laugh. "As far as I recall, you were the lead researcher in that facility. All authority over the experiments belonged to *you*. Even here—" He nodded to the corridor behind him without taking his eyes off Julio. "I see you have kept up with your dirty hobby."

"Do you believe any noble could fund my research?" Julio sneered and pointed at the prince. "I received an imperial pardon to study the mages and their awakening process."

Thessian's vision clouded with red. "You are lying!"

He advanced on Julio when, suddenly, their surroundings trembled with an animalistic roar.

Thessian half-turned, searching for the cause of the disturbance.

Julio squeezed past him and launched out of the room.

Spitting out a curse, Thessian charged after him.

At the end of a long corridor, Julio slipped into a dark hole in the wall that seemed to be an unfinished passageway.

With his large body, Thessian climbed through the hole. He nearly tripped on a pile of rocks nearby. Once he was certain he had his footing under control, he resumed the chase and followed the echoing sound of Julio's footsteps.

Thessian arrived in a cavern that had a single drawbridge on his side.

Upon seeing the prince, Julio panicked and kept yanking at the drawbridge's lever that would not budge.

"You are not going anywhere!" Thessian shouted.

On the other side of the pit, he spied Laurence and Lady Riga, ready to intercept their target if the bridge came down.

Julio let out a squeak like a cornered animal. He had nowhere left to run. With Thessian's approach, the scientist backed away towards the edge of the dark pit.

"You may not believe me, but my words are true. The one responsible for funding my research is none other than your father. H-How do you think I escaped? His men released me and gave me a new identity."

Thessian's hands trembled at his sides. His grip on the hilt of his sword grew painful.

Father would never do something so disgusting! He must be lying.

Julio gingerly pointed towards the passage. "In my office, you will find evidence. I have a letter with the emperor's seal on it."

A deep frown set on Thessian's forehead. His father had a unique seal, the location of which was only known to the owner. Thessian and his brothers had once made a bet where the person who found it would get the white mare their father bought for them from Shaeban.

None of them succeeded.

"And what were you doing in Dante?" Thessian growled, taking a menacing step forward.

"I was just—" Julio's foot slipped, and he lost his balance. His eyes bulged as he fell backwards into the endless darkness.

On instinct, Thessian rushed in, trying to catch him with no success.

A single scream of terror bounced off the walls of the cavern until everything went silent.

Could Julio survive such a fall?

"Your Highness!" Laurence yelled from across the pit. "Lower the bridge!"

Thessian shook off the unpleasant feeling in his gut and walked over to the lever that Julio had previously struggled with. He put all his strength into moving it.

His mind wandered as the bridge's chains clattered down, its wooden bulk landing with a dull thud. He let go and waited for the others to join him on his side of the pit.

"That was Julio Grande, was it not?" Laurence asked, peering over the edge.

Thessian gave a sharp nod.

"What did he say?"

As Thessian opened his mouth to speak, another violent tremor passed through the cavern.

Heavy rocks fell from the ceiling and landed a short distance away from them.

Lady Riga looked around nervously. "We should not stay here for much longer..."

Thessian pointed over his shoulder. "We must find out what is causing these tremors."

He dismissed Riga's incredulous look and started running in the direction of the central chamber.

26

OVERGROWN LIZARD

EMILIA

Emilia had no more time to argue with Clayton. She took a deep breath, trying to calm her racing heart. Stepping out from behind a thick pillar, she faced the scaly monster with fierce determination. She kept a straight face while her stomach was doing somersaults from worry.

Shiny charcoal scales covered the towering monster from head to toe. Its claws and teeth seemed sharp enough to slice through iron.

The beast's golden eyes, which had a slight glow to them, observed her with apparent curiosity.

Emilia gingerly raised her hands to show she had no weapons. "Greetings, mighty dragon."

When it didn't immediately attack, she inched forward. She stayed close to the safety of the pillar in case she needed to make a dive for it.

"Can you understand the language of this kingdom?"

The dragon mimicked her by getting closer.

She bit her lip. *I can't believe I am talking to a dragon. What if this is an overgrown lizard and not some mythical beast?*

Oh gosh, oh gosh, oh gosh!

With another step from the dragon, she fought the desire to turn tail and run. Her danger meter was screaming at her to escape. Despite her reluctance, she knew she had to deal with the dragon under her castle. That thing could rip the catacombs apart and bury her, along with her allies, in the rubble. She needed a plan to contain it.

Her eyes briefly zeroed in on the cage it had destroyed.

Was it willing to stay shackled and caged all this time? How do I make it go back to its humanoid form?

"How about we discuss matters at eye level?" she suggested. "We could speak upstairs, in a fine dining hall, instead of this dusty old place."

The beast ignored her attempt at communication. It leaned back onto its hind legs and let out a roar loud enough to deafen everyone present in the central chamber.

She instinctively covered her ears and glided back.

Clayton jumped in front of her. Over his shoulder, he said, "Your Majesty, please retreat."

The dragon's throat glowed with an intense heat, visible even through its tough scales.

"Get out of the way, Clayton!" Emilia screamed.

It was too late.

A large ball of fire erupted from the dragon's throat and propelled toward them.

Clayton hugged Emilia so tight that her nose ended up slamming into his solid chest.

She stuck her head up to complain.

Her words did not leave her mouth.

Clayton had erected a wall of ice behind him in the shape of huge wings. They were beautiful, but quickly cracked on impact with the scorching flames. Pain was etched all over his face, despite his best efforts to hide it, and his skin had lost its usual colour.

The smell of burning flesh hit her nose and, in an instant, she knew his back had taken significant damage.

Emilia grabbed him by the arm, mumbling an apology, and dragged him with what strength she had to the nearest pillar.

The dragon's flame died down, and its sharp eyes resumed their calculating assessment of her movements.

She overheard Laurence's gasp from the other end of the room. "Good gods, is that what I think it is?"

Without leaving the safety of the pillar, she shouted, "It's a dragon! Be careful!"

"Are you unharmed?" Thessian yelled back.

"For now."

The prince gave out orders to split up and prepare for a fight.

Emilia's attention returned to the man before her. Clayton did not look too well. Although he was a healing mage, she could tell his mana was depleted. He was on the brink of losing consciousness.

The remnants of the magical wings shattered, and chunks of ice fell around them.

Kneeling in front of him, she cupped his cheek and gave it a few soft taps.

"Clayton? Can you get up? We need to move while the others distract the beast."

He grumbled something unintelligible.

Another roar came from the dragon, making her check on the situation.

The beast was chasing Laurence and snapping its devastating jaws.

Thessian had his sword in hand and used one pillar for protection while Lady Riga commenced forming a fireball next to him.

"I guess Laurence is playing decoy."

Emilia draped Clayton's arm over her shoulders and wrapped her free arm around his waist.

His back was soaked with sweat or blood, or both.

Best not to think too hard about it.

She struggled to get up with the weight of a muscular, six-foot-tall man on her. No matter how much muscle training she did in the past, an unconscious man was still on par in weight with a large fallen tree.

Her legs trembled under the pressure.

With each shaky step towards the exit, she prayed Laurence would keep the dragon at bay long enough for them to slip away.

Out of the corner of her eye, she saw Riga's fireball flying at the dragon's head.

It let out a pained cry and instantly redirected its attention to the young mage.

Thessian's and Emilia's eyes met.

The prince took in the situation and, without a word, nodded before he ran at the beast with a sword in hand.

Emilia's lips tugged into a faint smile. *He's a hero to the end.*

Ignoring the commotion behind her, she shuffled out of the central chamber.

"You can do this, Emilia." She told herself and focused on moving one foot in front of the other. "One. Step. At. A. Time. You can go back to living the life you always wanted, with hot guys popping out left and ri—"

Her foot hit a stone, and she nearly fell flat on her face. The only thing stopping her was sheer will and a lot of cussing under her breath.

At the far end of the passageway, she spotted two figures getting closer.

Lionhart raised a lantern and motioned in Emilia's direction as he muttered something to Cali.

They picked up the pace; their faces full of worry as they got closer.

Lifting Clayton's other arm over his shoulder and taking some of the weight off Emilia, Lionhart asked, "What happened back there? We felt tremors throughout the catacombs."

Emilia blew away some of her stray hair that had gotten into her eyes. "We encountered a problem."

"Where is His Highness? Is he hurt?" Cali pressed.

Emilia gestured towards the central chamber, tilting her head in that direction. "He is in there, fighting a dra—"

Before she could finish the word 'dragon', Dame Cali sprinted away.

Stunned, Emilia stared at Cali's shrinking form as the distance between them grew. "I hope she knows how to fight dragons."

Lionhart gave her a long stare. "Is there truly a dragon in there?"

"Would I lie about something like that?"

"I guess not."

Clayton let out a low grunt as she adjusted her posture.

"We should get this man to safety," Emilia suggested.

Lionhart gave a curt nod and shouldered most of Clayton's weight, which allowed Emilia a quick study of Clayton's back.

She let out a hiss.

His backside looked like a medium rare steak. His tattoo became a mess of blood, charred skin, and raw flesh.

Her stomach churned. *I shouldn't have looked...*

Lionhart led the way back through the passageways, inquiring about the ongoings that led to the dragon's release.

"So, ultimately, you released the dragon," Lionhart commented matter-of-factly.

Emilia grimaced. "How was I supposed to know that a child could turn into a dragon?"

"To suppress a beast so powerful, the shackles would have had magic-nullifying runes carved into them."

"I may have read the books in the Royal Library, but there were no books on magic in there. King Gilebert did his best to hide this creature from everyone, including his children."

"I am not blaming you, Emilia."

Clayton remained unconscious as they climbed the stairs to the hidden entrance in the west wing.

Lionhart narrowed his eyes on the assassin. "Clayton did not notice anything was amiss until it was too late. I blame him."

"Do not be too hard on him. He protected me with his body."

"As any obedient dog should when its owner is in danger."

She cringed at her mentor's harsh words. Clayton was not a mere pawn to discard at a moment's notice. He put in great effort to complete the missions she had given him and even risked his life to protect her.

Her chest tightened as she struggled to understand the unexpected feeling that had taken hold of her.

Why am I so concerned over a single character's well-being when he is nothing but an unknown extra?

"We are almost there." Lionhart's words drew Emilia out of her reverie as he pulled on a lever to unlock the secret door panel. "Let's go to the infirmary."

"We should hurry."

27

MIXED FEELINGS

L A U R E N C E

Laurence ducked behind a stone pillar and gasped for air. His heart pounded loud enough in his head that it dulled the constant questions summoned by his restless mind.

That is a dragon. A real. Live. Dragon!

"I have its attention!" Thessian hollered.

Laurence swallowed his nerves and left his cover. He held his sword in an unrelenting grip. Losing a weapon in a battle against such a monster would be an instant death sentence. Ice wolves and hobgoblins were nothing compared to a beast that could grow as big as a castle. Be it luck on their side or the timing, they discovered the dragon before it reached maturity. Young dragons were arrogant and made plenty of mistakes.

He ran as quickly as his legs could carry him to one of the dragon's hind legs. Just as he was about to plunge his sword into its scaled flesh, it turned and swung its tail at him.

Laurence jumped back, yet a part of the tail collided with his chest, sending him flying backwards and landing hard on his posterior.

The dragon turned its attention to Laurence and screeched.

Lady Riga ran over, blocking the dragon's view with a forming ball of fire. The flame seemed unstable, and her hands were shaking. She lifted the misshapen flames above her head and launched them at the enemy. Then she quickly captured Laurence by the lapels of his jacket and attempted to pull him up.

"Get up, Sir Laurence!" she pleaded.

Laurence did not need to be told twice. He scrambled to his feet and took her hand in his.

They ran to the nearest pillar for shelter as His Highness attacked the distracted dragon from the side.

Upon closer inspection, Laurence noted Riga's pale complexion. She was panting, and her small hands trembled at her sides.

"How much mana do you have left?"

She straightened her posture, but he could see fear taking root in her eyes. "Not much."

"There is no way we can defeat it. No matter how distracted it is, it seems to always react as if it can read our minds." He stilled as he remembered crucial information from his days at the Hellion Imperial Academy. "Wait here, Lady Riga."

Laurence stuck his head around the edge of the pillar and yelled, "The dragon can read our minds, Your Highness!"

Thessian parried the dragon's swipe.

Without looking at Laurence, the prince snapped, "I need a distraction!"

"I will do it!" Cali shouted as she ran into the chamber with her shortsword and dagger in hand.

Calithea threw the dagger at the dragon's forehead. The blade bounced off the hard scales but forced the beast to turn its head in her direction long enough for Thessian to get out of its attacking range.

Laurence followed Cali's lead and took out his dagger from the sheath in his right boot. He waited until the dragon encroached on Cali to aim at the monster's neck, where the scales were supposed to be the weakest.

As he stepped out of his cover, the dragon changed direction to where Laurence was.

The beast truly CAN read our minds.

Even with such a powerful ability as mind-reading, there was no way the dragon could fight against four opponents at once.

Lady Riga nodded to Laurence and ran out, firing multiple small fireballs at the dragon's eyes in quick succession.

Cali and Thessian got close enough to the target to stab their swords into the beast's hind legs.

As the dragon swung its long tail to protect itself, Laurence saw his chance and threw his dagger with all his might.

"Come on, Lady Luck! Please be a hit!" Laurence mumbled.

The dagger lodged in the dragon's neck, and the monster roared in pain. The sound of its warning screech reverberated through the air as it swung its tail, causing the party to scatter towards the safety of the pillars.

The dragon turned towards the main entrance and bolted.

"It's trying to run away," Thessian announced. "Follow it!"

Laurence glanced at the young mage, who was barely standing. "Your Highness, Lady Riga needs to rest."

The prince pointed to Calithea. "Cali, bring the young lady back to the palace. Laurence and I will give chase."

"Understood, Your Highness." Cali walked over to Riga and went down on one knee. "Are you well enough to walk?"

Riga shook her head.

Cali turned around and offered her back. "Please climb on, my lady."

The child slumped on Cali's back without protest.

Thessian grasped Laurence's shoulder and lowered his voice. "We must get the dragon away from the palace and the city. We may need to act as bait until we are a safe distance away."

"You cannot be serious, Your Highness! With a mind-reading ability, it is impossible to fight a dragon with only two people."

Laurence spared a glance at the ladies. He could not let them be in any more danger. "Do you have a plan?"

"We will have to think of one on the way." Thessian motioned for Laurence to follow.

Laurence was willing to give up his life for Thessian. He never regretted his decision, as doing so meant he could be by his best friend's side and keep him safe.

This is one tale that won't require embellishing.

With a cocky smirk firmly in place, Laurence trailed after the prince.

No matter how long they scoured the catacombs for the dragon, they could not find it anywhere. Laurence suspected it had shape-shifted to get away from pursuers. Even the tracks had vanished once the passageways became too tight for the beast's full body.

Laurence wiped at his sweaty forehead with the back of his sleeve. "We should give up. I believe it is no longer here."

Thessian did not seem happy. "You may be right. We should return to the central chamber."

"Why? Can we not head back to the palace where a hot bath and a hearty meal await our exhausted selves?"

"Then you go back while I retrieve something from Julio's study."

Laurence scowled. "What did he say before falling into the pit?"

Thessian came to a stop. The flickering light from the lantern he was holding distorted his expression. "He claimed my father gave him permission to study the awakenings of mages."

"That's preposterous!" Laurence raked his fingers through his messy hair. "The emperor would never do something so vile."

"Um…"

Laurence sensed his friend's inner turmoil and patted Thessian on the back. "Come now, there is no need to believe a cornered rat like Julio Grande. He was probably trying to distract you to make his escape."

"You may be right." Thessian did not sound convinced.

While they made their way back to the central chamber, silence fell upon them. For once, Laurence could not think of witty banter or a playful quip to distract his friend.

The discovery of Julio's research facility in Darkgate had the most severe impact on Thessian six years ago. The prince could not believe that someone from the Hellion Empire would willingly conduct experiments on children.

More than once, Laurence had nightmares from the sights he had witnessed first-hand. The children there had been physically and mentally tortured to the point of insanity and then dissected for a chance to gleam a little more. Ronne and Renne were among the newest additions to that facility and were the least affected. Yet, Laurence often wondered what kinds of scenes those twins had witnessed to join Thessian's army at the tender age of nine?

They reached the study Thessian had mentioned.

Laurence skimmed through some documents, spotting similar research he hoped would never see the light of day.

One look at the prince told him not to intervene as Thessian rummaged through the papers on the desk, throwing aside whatever he considered useless.

Laurence picked up a discarded parchment that caught his eye. It was a rough sketch of the magical shackles.

He read Julio's messy writing.

The restraints were used on the dragon hatchling after it shed the shell of the once dormant egg. Thereafter, the shackles were adjusted without removal to restrain the beast's growth and magical power.

He picked up another parchment. It detailed Julio's study of the dragon's growth. Whatever His Highness was searching for was not the information on the mythical beast.

Laurence folded the reports related to the dragon into his pocket. "Can I help you with anything?"

Thessian yanked a parchment off the desk. He scanned its contents in bitter silence.

Thessian's frown grew deeper with every line.

Laurence peered over the prince's shoulder, and his jaw nearly dropped to the floor. "Is that the seal of the emperor?"

Thessian nodded.

"Why would Julio Grande have something like that?"

"He admitted that the imperial family had commissioned his research. This seal is proof of that."

Laurence took a step back. "Could this be a forgery?"

"No." Thessian's eyes did not leave the dark red ink that was used to stamp the seal. "Father's seal has distinct characteristics, and they are all present. Also, the ink is the same as I have seen in his office."

"Someone could have—"

"This is a serious matter that must not leave this room." Thessian met Laurence's eyes as he stashed away the evidence. "I will speak with Father upon our return to the imperial capital. He is the only person who can shed light on this."

"What will we do with the dragon research that madman wrote?"

"Give it to Emilia. She may uncover more about what King Gilebert was up to if we give her those documents."

"Then I will gladly be your messenger boy and hand-deliver the information to her."

"You are still going north to find the beastmen."

"Blast! And here I hoped you would forget about that."

28
MANA POTIONS

EMILIA

Emilia had her back resting against the wall of the infirmary and her arms crossed. She tapped her index finger against her arm as she watched Benjamin applying a thick green-grey paste to Clayton's entire back. At least Clayton was not conscious to feel the pain.

She gritted her teeth. When he showed up in her bedchambers to pledge his loyalty, she decided to use him for his abilities. Now, guilt gnawed at her, making her question her resolve.

Lionhart marched in with Lady Isobelle. As a member of House Escariot and Lord Armel's sister, she deserved to be updated.

Isobelle took one look at her brother's face and did not waste any time. Pushing the physician aside, she pinched Clayton's arm hard enough to turn the skin bright red.

Clayton winced and peeled open his eyes. "Izzy?"

Isobelle jerked him into a sitting position on the bed. "Drink this."

The lady pulled out a vial of shimmering blue liquid from the inner pocket of her gown, uncorked it, and forced him to swallow the contents.

Emilia was ready to stop Lady Isobelle when Lionhart said, "Don't worry. That is a mana potion made by the mages of the Mage Assembly. It is an extremely expensive drug that will be of great help in this situation."

Satisfied her brother finished drinking, Isobelle tossed the empty bottle to the physician who barely caught it.

The lady slapped her hands to her hips. "Stop acting all pitiful in front of your master and heal yourself, Brother."

"I love you too, Izzy." With a low chuckle, Clayton closed his eyes. His body emitted a warm glow that made Emilia and the others squint.

Seeing someone heal such severe damage fascinated Emilia to no end.

The magic died down after ten minutes.

Clayton got up as if nothing happened and stretched.

From where Emilia stood, she could tell his back was back to normal, including the strange tattoo he sported.

Benjamin clapped in awe. "Lord Armel, how I wish I possessed even a smidgen of your healing power. I could save so many lives."

Clayton replied, "If that happened, the Church would hunt you, and you would not be able to work at the palace."

"Hmm." Benjamin appeared thoughtful and pushed his glasses up his nose. "You may be right, my lord." He looked at Emilia and then inclined his head in respect. "I believe there is nothing more for me to do. I shall return to my desk, Your Majesty."

"Thank you for your hard work," Emilia said.

"Nonsense. I did nothing." The physician's shoulders sagged, and he trudged towards his messy desk at the far end of the room.

Isobelle kicked her brother in the shin, causing him to double over. "You had me worried there! I have no plans to marry some old noble to retain the title."

Clayton hopped off the bed and hugged his sister close. "Thank you for worrying about me."

With a huff, Isobelle pushed her brother away. "Since everything is fine, I am planning to retire for the night. *Do not* call for me." As an afterthought, she curtsied to Emilia. "My harsh words only apply to my brother, Your Majesty. Feel free to call upon me day or night if I can be of service."

"You change your tune pretty quickly," Clayton commented.

Isobelle dismissed him with a wave of her hand and sashayed out of the room with a sway of her hips.

Emilia fought to keep a straight face.

Somehow, Isobelle lightened up the heavy atmosphere that had settled among them in a matter of minutes. One day, she wished to get better acquainted with Clayton's sister. Perhaps even become friends.

Yet, the positive mood did not last long. Emilia was still at fault for putting her people in danger.

Lionhart cleared his throat. "Your Majesty, I will return to the catacombs to check on the situation. Speak your mind when I am gone."

Emilia didn't have time to interject. Her spymaster escaped all too readily.

She let out a frustrated sigh. "I do not think I can apologise enough for my reckless actions that led to your injuries, Lord Armel."

"I do not blame you, Your Majesty."

She could not meet his eyes for fear that if she looked, she would see hatred and disapproval reflected in them.

Why do I care what he thinks of me? He is a subordinate, a tool, a killer...

He stepped closer. "Please look at me."

Emilia hesitated yet lifted her head.

Clayton had a soft smile on his handsome face.

She looked into his stormy-grey eyes, and they seemed to calm her anxious thoughts. What she saw confused her unsettled heart further.

How can he not blame me? I nearly got him killed!

"Clayton, I think it would be best if you live your life free of the palace. You no longer need to be a shadow for the Dante crown, for you have saved my life today."

He lowered himself to his knees and clasped her hand gently, as though it were something precious. The warmth of his touch sent a tingling sensation up her arm. "Even without my curse, I would be more than happy to serve you. That is why my family may choose our master."

"But you got hurt because of me!"

"And I would do it again." He looked at her with an unwavering gaze. "Please give me another chance! I will make sure not to get hurt or disappoint you again."

She grappled with her conscience. Her lips formed into a thin line as she pulled her hand out of his. "I will think on this some more. You have worked hard today, Lord Armel. I will have a servant bring you a change of clothes."

She made her way to the door. Placing her hand on the doorknob, his words stopped her.

"Do not abandon me, Your Majesty. You promised to help me break my family's curse."

Emilia did not turn around. "I intend to keep my word without forcing you to continue your work."

"I would prefer it if you use me."

How can he say such cheesy lines so easily?

"Rest well."

She walked out of the infirmary and closed the door behind her. With hurried steps, she made her way around the corner where she pressed her hand to her chest.

Her heart was racing.

Clayton was too big of a temptation when he was on his knees. If she wasn't careful, he could convince her to gamble her fortune away, and she would happily do it.

29
MISSING: DRAGON

THESSIAN

Thessian lifted a goblet of red wine to his lips. Taking a measured sip, he looked at the mesmerising view out of the arched, floor-to-ceiling window of his room.

The stars in the night sky shone brightly next to a bright half-moon.

Since he and Laurence resurfaced, there had been no trace of the dragon. The creature appeared smart enough to remain hidden while it healed its wounds. With a little luck, the dragon would forego taking its revenge on the kingdom that harmed him and leave Dante for good.

He finished his drink and placed the goblet on the marble mantelpiece.

A handful of the palace maids had prepared a bath for him a while ago.

He stripped out of his filthy clothes, tossing them near the copper bathtub for the servants to collect later.

Slowly, he sunk into the warm water.

A knock on the door had him rolling his eyes. *There is not even a moment of quiet for me these days.*

"Your Highness, are you sleeping?" It was the Queen.

He pulled himself out of the bathtub as the door opened, and Emilia stuck her head in.

Her eyes grew wide, and her cheeks turned a shade of the wine he had recently drank.

Emilia swiftly covered her face with her hands. "I did not mean to intrude. I just wanted—"

Thessian felt a wave of embarrassment warming his face. He grabbed a change of clothes off the chair next to the bathtub and hid behind a wooden screen to get dressed as quickly as was humanly possible. His clothes absorbed the remaining water on his body, making his white shirt stick to his skin.

Ignoring the discomfort, he opened the door wider for her. "Come in, Emilia."

She lowered her hands, taking a tentative peek at him. "Is it safe to look?"

"Would I open the door otherwise?"

"You are right. I was being silly." Her small face reddened for the second time.

Thessian cleared his throat. "Is there anything I can do for you at this late hour?"

She looked at him as if it was not uncommon for them to meet beyond polite hours.

Reflecting on the past, he recalled entering her bedchambers without invitation on numerous occasions. He wanted to kick his past self for an atrocious lack of manners. Having acted like such a mongrel, he had no right to complain.

Emilia glided into his room and waited until he closed the door to speak. "I saw the candlelight under the door and thought we could discuss some things."

"Sit anywhere you like."

She sat on the loveseat that was facing the lit fireplace.

Thessian followed close behind and sat next to her. Compared to her small frame, he seemed like a bear. He crossed his legs and folded his hands in his lap to make himself smaller.

"What can I do for you?"

Emilia was quiet. Her eyes focused on the orange flames dancing along the charred logs in the fireplace. "It is about the dragon. Lionhart and Dame Cali have ventured to the catacombs with the knights to track it. When Sir Laurence gave me Julio Grande's research notes, I searched the late king's study and bedchambers. I discovered a hidden journal. King Gilebert was eager to grow and kill the dragon to replenish the depleting Dragon's Heart mine in the north."

Thessian rubbed his jaw. "Is the jewel truly a part of the dragon's corpse?"

She let out a musical laugh. "Oh no. The king was an idiot to believe such a fantasy. Dragon's Heart is simply a rare deposit of eudialyte that grew rapidly due to the high quantities of mana in the area. It also changed some properties due to its location. I believe a dragon's death may have triggered the increase in mana, but its corpse would not have become a fancy gem."

"Do you think it is wise to tell me the secret of your country's gem?"

She shrugged. "I am nothing more than a stand-in until you become emperor and absorb Dante into the Hellion Empire."

He rubbed the back of his neck. Emilia did not seem attached to the Dante Kingdom. Her indifference was strange to him as he grew up with his tutors relentlessly drilling into him that he had to give his everything for the Empire.

"Do you hold no love for this land?"

Emilia fiddled with a signet ring on her middle finger. "I decided to be as open with you as I can, so I will answer. One day, I want to leave Dante. Nothing would make me happier than receiving a small fief where I can live out the rest of my days in comfort."

"What about marriage?"

"There is never a shortage of men seeking a wealthy bride."

He felt a smile tugging at his lips. "True. Nobles and commoners alike would gladly marry a wife who does not need any financial support."

"The second matter I wished to discuss is Duke Malette's trial. I plan to begin his formal trial as soon as possible." Emilia balled her hands in her lap. "He has quite a lot of sway among the nouveau riche and the royal faction as the former king's cousin. His territory is wealthy due to illegal mining practices and the sale of iron ore to the Reyniel Kingdom. If I wait for much longer, he may find a way to escape his sentence."

"Are you worried about the nobles and citizens seeing you as a tyrant?"

"Among the citizens, my reputation has been tarnished since birth," she said with a hint of sadness in her voice. "The Church of the Holy Light has made certain of it. This is why I have contacted His Holiness. I plan to trade Bishop Lagarde for the Church's acknowledgement and support of my coronation ceremony."

Thessian was taken aback by her bold plan. Not many rulers wanted to threaten the Church of the Holy Light if most of their citizens subscribed to the Church's ideology and beliefs.

Until Emilia got what she wanted, she would need strong military protection. With the state of current affairs, the castle was operating with a minimal number of servants and knights. He could send in more of his soldiers, but such a move would give cause for the undecided nobles to alienate her.

There was also Count Baudelaire. Although the Count appeared to care a great deal about Emilia and the Dante kingdom, Thessian could not trust the man's words so easily.

And a dragon was on the loose somewhere…

"Your Highness?"

"I believe you will make the right decisions, Emilia. In the meantime, I think it would be a good idea to leave the tracking of the dragon to Count Fournier. He is an experienced hunter, and his men have a wealth of knowledge in fighting monsters." He nodded to himself, pleased with his decision. "I will send him a missive explaining the situation."

"Please do not reveal to him about the dragon's origins or the catacombs."

He rubbed his stubbly jaw. "He is not a noble who is eager for the throne. Giving him as much information as possible regarding the dragon would be in our best interest."

"Human nature is hard to predict," she replied with a shake of her head. "You must remember that Count Fournier and the other nobles eagerly supported an invasion by a foreign power."

"I...will consider my words carefully."

She got up and inclined her head. "Thank you. That is everything that needed urgent attention. I will leave you to your bath. If you need more hot water, please notify the maids or Sir Rowell."

Thessian felt his ears burning as he watched her making her strategic exit.

He ran a hand over his face and sighed. Emilia was a seventeen-year-old queen who spent most of her life in the seclusion of a tower. Witnessing the sight of a naked man must have given her quite a shock.

30

HEAD MAID'S ADVICE

EMILIA

Emilia shut the door to her bedchambers behind her and ran over to her bed. She flopped face-first into the pillows and exhaled all of her embarrassment.

That's it! I am done with handsome men for the day.

A familiar knock on her door alerted her to Ambrose's presence.

The head maid walked in. "Your Majesty, I heard you were in danger in the catacombs. I should have accompanied you."

Reluctantly, Emilia pulled herself into a sitting position. She was still wearing dirt and blood-stained clothes that no longer resembled the elegantly tailored attire she had donned hours prior. Some time ago, her hair must have come undone from its ribbon as it fell around her face like a dark curtain.

"Ambrose, answer me this. Are all men in this world well endowed?"

Ambrose blinked slowly as if the question was being processed on an ancient computer. Her face went from neutral to angry, and she stormed over.

Taking Emilia's hands in hers, she demanded, "Who dared to defile Your Majesty's eyes with such disgusting imagery? Tell me who it was, and I will skin him alive. No. I will cut his—"

Emilia covered Ambrose's mouth, leaving the tirade unfinished. "There is no need to do that!"

Ambrose leaned back to speak. "But such filthy behaviour cannot go unpunished. The least I can do is have that monster hanged, drawn, and quartered."

"It was my fault in the first place."

"How can Your Majesty be at fault? Wait, was it Lord Armel? Did you see it when he was getting treatment?" Ambrose appeared conflicted as her brows drew together. "No. Even him, I cannot forgive. He may not have been conscious, but then it was Benjamin's fault. I will have a word with that useless physician."

Emilia caught Ambrose by the wrist, stopping her from leaving. "It was merely a hypothetical question, I swear. I—I recalled an old drawing of a man in one of the books in the Royal Library."

"Oh." Tension finally left Ambrose's shoulders. "Please tell me which book it was. I think it would be best to burn it in case someone else is scarred for life by its blasphemous content."

Laughter burst from deep within Emilia's chest. She wiped at the corners of her eyes when she felt tears welling up there. "I should have a bath after my adventure."

"I will have it prepared for you immediately and have the maids change your sheets, Your Majesty."

"Thank you, Ambrose."

"I am just fulfilling my duty."

A little later, Ambrose came back into the room with two maids who rushed off to prepare a hot bath. In the meantime, Ambrose helped undress Emilia to her undergarments.

Ambrose whispered next to Emilia, "To answer your question, Your Majesty, as far as I was told by my mother, not all men are created equal. It is unlikely that many of them in this kingdom possess an appendage larger than my middle finger. So, if you wish to keep a husband or a lover, make sure he is of use down there."

Emilia lowered her head to hide her flushed face. She did not expect an answer from her maid after how Ambrose reacted to the question. "I see."

"Make certain to tell me if there is a man you are interested in. Lionhart and I will do our best to dig up all of his dark secrets before you can grow your affection. Should he be deemed unsuitable, we will quietly take care of him."

"That is quite worrisome." Emilia chuckled. "I may end up with no suitors at all."

"That cannot be, Your Majesty," Ambrose assured her. "He merely has to be subservient to you, be extremely wealthy, be strong enough to protect you, and sacrifice himself should there be a need for it. Your Majesty deserves nothing less."

The maids who had prepared the bath bowed their heads low.

One of them spoke up. "Your Majesty, the bath is ready. Please enjoy it while we change the bedding."

"Quit idling!" Ambrose ordered them.

The duo visibly jumped at the harshness in Ambrose's tone and scrambled towards the bed.

Glad that Emilia was on Ambrose's good side, she made her way to the bath, where she relaxed and let go of the stress she had accumulated throughout the day. From the great fire in her city to discovering of a mythical creature under her castle, she had many things to worry about.

She sighed. *All of it can wait until tomorrow.*

31

AN UNEASY HEART

LAURENCE

Two days with almost no rest and constant physical activity had caught up with Laurence. He dragged his feet to one of the beds in the knights' quarters and collapsed on its rough surface. With Cali in charge of the place and most of them out on duty or in the catacombs, the chance of him getting into trouble was minuscule.

Laurence rolled onto his back. Staring at the wooden beams high above his head, he counted numerous decaying spider webs. The smell of sweat and sword oil hung thick in the air, reminding him of the days he spent with Thessian on the battlefield. The current times were comparatively peaceful, and he no longer needed to witness his comrades perishing by his side.

As a soldier loyal to the prince, all he had to do was follow orders. He could not envision the weight of the decisions that His Highness had to shoulder while sacrificing hundreds of his men to win battles. And now that Laurence was expelled from the unit until he could redeem himself, he felt like there was a gaping hole in his chest.

At some point, he must have fallen asleep as the next thing he saw was a knight's helmet above his face.

Laurence jerked into a sitting position and clutched at his spinning head. "What? Who?"

Cali's soft voice soothed his panic. "It's me, sir."

With a groan, he asked, "When did you return?"

"Not too long ago."

He noticed that no one else had entered the knights' quarters. "Did something happen? Where are the other knights?"

"I asked them to wait outside." Cali removed her helmet, making her shoulder-length blonde hair fall like a wave of golden straw. She placed her helmet on the nearby bed and wiped at the sweat on her forehead with her gloved hand.

"Should you require more sleep, sir, you may stay upstairs in my quarters."

After letting his frustrations out on her before, he stared at her blank expression. "Are you not mad at me for how I acted towards you?"

"I cannot be mad at the truth. Sir Laurence is much more fitting for the role of His Highness' second-in-command. I am merely filling in until you return from your mission."

As a commoner who became a royal knight and rose to such a high position, Calithea should be jumping for joy and boasting to her fellow friends. Seeing her doubting her abilities to such an extent gave him a bitter taste in his mouth.

He clambered off the bed and indicated in the direction of the stairs over his shoulder. "Tell your men to come in and rest. They must be tired after scouring the catacombs all night. I will take you up on your offer and check out the quality of the Guard Captain's quarters."

She smiled so brightly that his heart skipped a beat. "I will be right up. There should still be some good ale left in my room."

Laurence hurried to the stairs. Taking two at a time to reach the top, he spotted the room at the end of the gloomy and dusty hallway. He made his way inside and sucked in a lungful of air. There had to be some kind of mistake. His treacherous heart reacted to his comrade out of the blue.

Trying to distract himself, he walked around her plain room.

Cali had a single wooden desk which appeared to be well-organised. Everything seemed to have its place, from the parchments to the ink pot and quill. The bed was made, and the aged oak dresser did not have a single sign of dust on it. Even the floor was too clean for a room where men in dirty boots would occasionally visit.

In the years they had trained together, he knew from her swordsmanship that Cali was meticulous and hard-working. She never complained about the toughness of the training or the missions assigned to her. There was more than one occasion where he wondered if she was capable of expressing her dissatisfaction at all.

He heard her steps on the stairs and decided to sit on the chair at her desk. Taking up her bed would be rude even for him.

She beamed once again when she saw him. "Sir Laurence, I am finished with my duties. Would you like to have a drink with me?"

"I will never say no to good alcohol."

Cali closed the door behind her and began stripping her armour off.

Laurence faced away.

As if to answer his sudden discomfort, she added, "It would be uncomfortable to wear full armour."

From the corner of his eye, he saw her removing the breastplate and pulling it over her head. Underneath, her baggy linen shirt hid her slim figure as the material found more freedom.

Once the last piece of steel armour was removed, she stood there in a tight pair of trousers and a grey shirt. Cali secured her hair into a ponytail. She unlocked a small storage chest by her bed and pulled out a bottle of Newburn ale.

With a bottle in one hand, she brought over two goblets which she placed on her desk.

"Please pour the drinks while I wash up, Sir Laurence."

He nodded, eager to get his nerves under control with alcohol. Once his goblet was filled to the brim, he downed it in one go. The sweet and fruity taste had little similarity to the alcohol of the Hellion Empire.

After a series of terrible events, he let out a long sigh and continued to consume drink after drink.

Sometime later, the door creaked open.

Through blurry vision, he made out a gorgeous blonde, who resembled Calithea, in a white linen shirt. His eyes roamed her slender body, and he swallowed loudly.

As if concerned for him, she rushed to his side and cupped his face. "Sir, are you already inebriated? What about me?" She glanced at the empty bottle on the desk. "I see it was quite strong."

"I am very strong!" he claimed with a sluggish smile. "You can see how strong by taking a seat on my lap."

He grabbed her around the waist and pulled her down. Once she was securely sitting on his thighs, he buried his face in her neck and inhaled the soothing smell of soap.

"You smell divine, my beautiful fairy."

She let out a giggle and wrapped her arms around his shoulders. "Sir, you might regret this when you sober up, but would you like to spend the rest of the night with me?"

"Of course! There is no better place than in your embrace."

He nuzzled his nose against her smooth cheek before kissing her with great fervour.

Her lips moved in a shy and inexperienced way. Every so often, he had to pause as she pulled back to gasp for air.

Even inebriated, he would not force himself on a lady. Since she had come to him willingly, he would take things slow and make her enjoy their time together. After all, he had never left a woman unsatisfied. They could say he was a player but not a lousy lover.

How long had it been since he had a woman's body against his? Too long, it seemed, because not even the liquor could soften the hardness he sported against her thighs. He wanted to devour her, but she was on top of him, covering his face with kisses.

One should not rush a goddess like her.

"I shall be patient," he slurred as his hands moved down her slim waist to her tight buttocks.

She pulled back and asked sweetly, "Don't you find me attractive, sir?"

"You're one of the most beautiful women I've ever seen!" *Albeit a bit blurry.*

The blonde shifted on his lap and did not reply.

"What is the matter?"

For a moment, he believed that she was pouting. He grabbed her chin and brought her mouth against his. "You have my full attention, beautiful."

"Sir, do you want to follow me to my bed?"

Laurence combed his fingers through her soft, golden locks. "Yes. A bed would be more suitable for what we are about to do."

Laurence grumbled under his breath as sunlight from the window invaded the room. He tried to escape it by rolling away from the dastardly brightness. Burrowing his face in the soft bosom of a lady was the best feeling in the world. He relaxed as he recalled the passionate night he spent with a woman. No. Not a mere woman. A goddess who could match his stamina.

Despite the raging hangover that quickly surfaced, his eyes snapped open.

Blonde woman? Bed?

Dread clawed its way into his heart, and his stomach dropped.

Laurence's last memory was of him being in the knights' quarters with none other than Dame Calithea Louberte.

He propelled himself off the bed, stark naked, and stared in horror at the dishevelled appearance of his comrade. His mouth refused to close. The shock was too much for his hungover brain to handle.

Cali's toned, sun-kissed body was half-covered with a sheet. She sat up, rubbing her eyes. "Sir Laurence? Is everything alright?"

Laurence staggered backwards until his back hit a wall. He looked down and covered his crown jewels with his hands.

"How? But I was with—Well, I mean... I-I think I should go..."

Her expression soured. "If you leave in your state of undress, you will find yourself quite embarrassed later."

He nodded vigorously.

"Yes! Clothes! I—err..." He scanned the room for his belongings and, lightning-fast, donned them, almost falling twice in the process. "Cali, I—"

"We will speak about this later." She covered her exposed chest with the sheets. "I have training drills to oversee."

"Ye-yes..." He wiped at his sweaty forehead and backed out of the room.

His heart was in his throat, and his legs shook as if he was carrying a horse on his back.

Somehow, he managed to get to the garden where he slumped on the stone bench and let out a flurry of curses in his native tongue. He broke his cardinal rule to never get involved with his female subordinates.

Pausing, he blankly stared at the naked statues at the centre of the fountain.

Cali was no longer his subordinate. Rather, he was below her in rank since he made a mess of the city.

"No, this is still a huge problem!" He scratched his head with his hands as if it would shake some knowledge loose in his fogged-up brain. "It's Cali! How could I do that to someone like her?"

Cold sweat formed on his back with a chilling thought.

What if I forced her? She treats me as her superior despite the demotion. Did she feel obligated to sleep with me?

Laurence raked his fuzzy memories. He did not imagine Calithea returning his kisses or enjoying their passionate night.

Laurence, you fool! Even if you were drunk, you should have known better!

Cursing yet again, he shot upright.

"I need advice! Do I take responsibility? Do I apologise first? How much do rings cost?"

Mother will kill me.

TO BE CØNTINUED ...

LANGUAGE OF THE BEASTMEN

Here are some of the phrases Khaja has used in this book:

"Vas ntes tietna, kaiedes i aunen!" - You are animals, like the rest.

"Vosie ntes mir, arikesh. Jya otarkert vosie." - You are mine, hindwalker. I marked you.

"Jya ne fera werst vosie hedu, arikesh." - I will not kill you today, hindwalker.

"Oin zaotuo yille eund dei arikeshe. Jya mopeca emberh vas." - One pointed ear and two hindwalkers. I can take you.

"Jya werst vosie ointes, arikesh." - I kill you first, hindwalker.

"Jya delte ankota. Osie kablenen fabise." - I should attack. They seem weak.

"Wo sohen raci?" - We go out here?

BEASTMEN DICTIONARY (TO DATE)

Words and their meaning:

Jya - I
Vosie – (singular) You
Vas – (plural) You
Wo – we
Osie – they
Mir – mine
Moin – my
Nare – our
Vast – is
Ntes – are
Eund – and
I – the
Kur – to
Ne – not/no
Da – yes
Mopeca – can
Delte – should
Deche – make
Emberh – take
Kablenen - seem\appear
Oin - one
Dei – two
Ointes – first
Deites – second
Hedu - today
Redu - yesterday
Indu – tomorrow
Kaiedes – like (similar to, hold affection for)
Tietna – animals
Aunen – the rest, others
Zaotuo – pointed, sharp, protruding

Yille – ear
Arikeshe – (plural) hindwalkers, a term used for humans
Arikesh – (singular) hindwalker
Werst – kill
Ukiy – hard
Ankota – attack
Heslich – happy
Fabise – weak
Sohen – go, go out, leave through
Raci – here
Paci – there
Fera – will, planning to do something
Ne fera – not will (won't)
Otarkert – marked
Zaregh – capture
Golnad – big, large
Kadachek – gift
Tsessen – kiss, kissing
Sier – bond
Nur – for
Vibezn – life
Varetz - Father

ABOUT THE AUTHOR

May Freighter is an award-winning, internationally bestselling author from Ireland. She writes Fantasy, Urban Fantasy, Paranormal Romance, and Sci-Fi Mysteries that will keep you entertained, mystified, and hopefully craving more. Currently, she's attempting to parent two little monsters and hasn't slept in over 4 years.

Who needs sleep these days, anyway?

On days when May can join her fictional characters on an adventure, stars must align in the sky and meteors will probably rain down. So, keep an eye out.

Her hobbies are photography, drawing, plotting different ways of characters' demise, and picking up toys after her kids. Not exactly in that order, either.

For more information about the author and their work, visit their website: **www.authormayfreighter.com**

FIND OUT WHAT HAPPENS NEXT IN:

With each passing day, life in Dante becomes more complicated.

The duke is on trial, Emilia's capital is slowly recovering from The Great Fire, and the treasury is almost depleted. To make matters worse, her servants keep misunderstanding her relationship with Prince Thessian. Add an attractive Pope with a smile to die for, and it's a recipe for disaster waiting to happen.

What doesn't help is that the dragon is still missing, and Sir Laurence seems to be a trouble magnet no matter where he goes.

As the side quests keep piling up, Emilia is forced to put her dream life on hold and possibly explore her feelings for a man who's willing to do anything for her.

Yet, the enemies of the Crown never sit still. With new sinister plans in motion, the lives of Emilia's subjects are at stake, and when Thessian falls into grave danger, the young queen is forced to make a choice that could bring about the destruction of her kingdom.

Printed in Great Britain
by Amazon

52bce35a-98d1-450a-a7c9-0c3edbcfe7c8R01